Zoe Price lives with her husband and daughter in a village just inside the Welsh border. She has a small black dog called Rose which she enjoys walks with.

When she is not writing she is reading or watching the latest Marvel and Star Wars films/TV series.

Christmas films are also a favourite of hers as this is her favourite time of year. Her favourite Christmas film has got to be *Santa Claus the Movie*, David Huddleston is the best Santa in her opinion. She also loves decorating for Christmas.

For Dave, without whom this book would not be possible.

Zoe Price

CHRISTMAS WISHES IN MISTLETOE

AUSTIN MACAULEY PUBLISHERS™

LONDON • CAMBRIDGE • NEW YORK • SHARJAH

A CIP catalogue record for this title is available from the British Library.

ISBN 9781035811748 (Paperback)
ISBN 9781035811755 (ePub e-book)

www.austinmacauley.com

First Published 2023
Austin Macauley Publishers Ltd®
1 Canada Square
Canary Wharf
London
E14 5AA

I would like to thank my husband for all his support and encouragement, and my daughter for making me smile every day.

A big thank you to my mum who gave me her honest opinion on my novel and gave me hope that it will be liked by others.

Thank you to the amazing team at Austin Macauley for all their help and support. Thank you for believing in me and making my dream come true.

I would also like to thank you, reader, as without you I couldn't live my dream.

Chapter One

I have finally made my mind up about a life-changing decision I have been contemplating with since the news of my impending redundancy. It's not all bad, though. I'm getting a generous severance package from my event manager position, which is the only reason I can do what I have planned. The company I'm working for is merging with another small company, which is leaving only one manager job available, which has gone to Sally. She does have more experience than I do, but I'm still gutted about it.

I've worked my way up the ladder from school and love my job. It doesn't even feel like a job as I love it so much, but at the same time it has given me this chance of a lifetime. It's time to make one of my lifelong dreams come true. All I have to do now is to tell Mum about it. This is really hard, as I know Mum will have concerns over the whole thing, but this feels like the right time for me to do this. If I don't do it now, then I never will, and at the moment I have no commitments with work and life in general, it's the perfect time to go.

I've just made Mum a cup of tea, and we sit at the dining table. I have even brought a cake to help soften the blow, as I know Mum will be apprehensive about it. Plus, cake always makes everything feel better. Here goes nothing.

"Mum, I've decided to go to America for three weeks. For Christmas." Getting it all out in one go. I can see the concern all over her face.

"Are you sure? Have you thought it through?"

"Yes, Mum, I'm sure." I made sure to sound positive to reassure her that I have given this a lot of thought.

"On your own, though?"

"Yes, on my own. I need to do this, and since I have been made redundant, it is the perfect time to go. I've got a great redundancy package and some savings. I won't be completely on my own; there will be other guests there for Christmas. Plus, lots of activities that I will be able to join in." I knew she would cling to that aspect of it, and it is scary going on my own, but I'm not going to let that stop me.

"You've talked about it for so long, but I didn't think you would do it. Especially on your own."

"I don't need a man to be able to do this. I am thirty-one years old, and as you just said, it is something I have always wanted to do. Now feels like the right time." I understand her hesitance about this, but Mum has known it has been a dream for mine for years. Can't she see how excited I am to be going. I want her to be happy for me, as she is always telling us to follow our dreams and hearts.

"I'm happy you are following your dreams. I'm just worried about you out there all on your own. I will miss you loads. You have to keep checking in with me, so I know you are OK." Mum gives me a reassuring hug. I know she doesn't want to stand in my way or hold me back.

"I will miss you too, Mum, and I will keep in touch and send you lots of photos. It's three weeks. I'll soon be back." I gave Mum a big hug to help her feel happier.

We finished our tea and cake and discussed all the things that I would do whilst I was there. How I will get to see proper snow and not the small minuscule amount that we get here in

North Wales. I'm really excited about the trip, and I'm glad Mum can see that I am happy about making my dreams come true.

It has been one of my long-time dreams to go to America for Christmas, to experience it their way. I wasn't just going to go anywhere in America either, but a small town, just like the ones you see in the Christmas films that I love watching every year. I've done a lot of research and exploring the Internet, and came across a town called Mistletoe, which seems perfect. It even has a Christmas-themed name. I love it. It is situated deep in northern Vermont. It has a beautiful wooden inn, and the town looks spectacular in the photos, all done up for Christmas. I can't wait to see it all in person. There is lots going on in the small town too that I will be able to take part in, including a parade and a party at the inn on Christmas Eve. Plus, the New Year's Eve party that the town is holding. I am looking forward to it all, especially the atmosphere.

I've always loved Christmas and since watching Hallmark Christmas films and reading my fair share of Christmas books. I have dreamed about experiencing a Christmas, just like those ones. With the small town, snow, Christmas markets and festivities, I can't believe that I am finally going, and in a town that looks just like the films and books describe. I'm glad that I got past the fear of going on my own, as I'm not going to let being single stop me from going. You don't need a man to be able to live out your dreams. The way I see it, it means that I would be able to join in as many activities that I want to with no one holding me back. I'm going to have the time of my life, and I know I won't get this opportunity again.

I'm also not going to let the fact that I don't have a job to come back to worry me; it is something that I can deal with in the new year. After working at events since I was eighteen and working my way up to manager, I'm pretty confident that I will find something when I get back. I had thought about looking for a job straight away but decided that with the redundancy money that I would finally go to America. After working so hard over the last 13 years, I'm extremely thankful for this opportunity.

I spent the next couple of weeks finishing up at work and sorting through which clothes to take. Mistletoe is going to be colder than it is here in Wales, so I've had to do some shopping for warmer clothes. I enjoyed selecting winter accessories, and it made for a perfect excuse to buy more shoes. I will need a decent pair for walking in snow after all. I also made sure I had a few Christmas jumpers with me and some warm pyjamas. When I finished packing, I ended up having one big case, one small case and a carry-on case along with my handbag. It seems like a lot, but it is for three weeks and in cold weather, so my clothes are bulkier, making less room in the cases. At least that is what I'm telling myself.

I did all my Christmas shopping and wrapped it all, as I don't want my family missing out on their gifts on Christmas day. With me going on 12th December and not returning till 2nd January, the family have planned a Christmas lunch the day before I fly out. This is when they plan to give me their Christmas gifts. Most gifts turned out to be dollars for me to take with me as some extra spending money. It was an emotional day, but it was great to have the traditional family Christmas with the big roast and all the trimmings, even it was fourteen days until the big day. It made me feel like I wouldn't be missing my traditions—just making memories that I would be able to cherish forever. I went to bed on a high from the celebrations. It feels just like Christmas Eve with the anticipation of my travels in the morning.

#

Chapter Two

I woke up feeling ecstatic; it feels just like Christmas morning. I did think that I would be feeling nervous about flying on my own, but I'm far too happy to have room for nerves. I get myself ready quickly, as I don't want to be running late. It is going to be a long day, as it is with two connecting flights to take me to Burlington International Airport, but it is definitely going to be worth it.

I'm all prepared for the long journey with a book in my hand luggage. Plus, I know I need to try and sleep for part of the journey. I need to get my body used to the time difference so that I don't lose any time while I'm there sleeping in the day. I don't want to be beaten by the jetlag. From Burlington, I will need to get a taxi into Mistletoe. It's not too far, and there is no way I would rent a car. They drive on the other side of the road. I'd be worried about being on the wrong side all the time. It's another tearful goodbye with the family, which I expected it would be. I give my mum one last hug goodbye, promising to keep in touch and to send pictures. Now that I'm on my way, though, some nerves have started to kick in, but I push them away so that I can enjoy every second of the journey.

#

Having just arrived at Burlington Airport, I instantly feel the difference in temperature. It's a lot colder than I imagined it to be. Don't get me wrong. I was expecting the coldness, but I had no idea it would be this bitter. My face is tingling with the cold. I'm so glad that I decided to travel in the new boots and my warmer clothes. Getting my hat and gloves out of my bag, another good decision, I go in search of a taxi. Happy that it doesn't take me long to find one. I'm feeling tired, and the sudden coldness has given me the shakes. I suppose I'll get used to the temperature difference. Well, I hope I do. I'll have to just put it out of my mind. The driver is friendly with that lovely accent. He puts my luggage in the boot, which I'm grateful for. I'm sure it's gotten heavier. I take my seat out of the cold.

"Where to, love?"

"Mistletoe, please."

"First time visiting?"

"Yes, it is. I've always wanted to experience an American Christmas." The smile on my face so big I must look like an idiot, but who cares.

"Thought that was an English accent. Are you staying in the inn?"

"Yes, how did you know?" I cautiously raise an eyebrow at him.

"Only two places to stay, figured I'd try the inn first, as that's always first choice for most," the driver replied with a smile, putting me at ease.

His friendly banter and warm smile has me feeling more relaxed. I'm glad to be on the last part of my journey. It's more tiring than you think. It's a short drive to the bridge that leads to Mistletoe. It has a wooden covering and is painted red, just like in the movies. I can't help but stare out the window admiring it. It adds to the Christmas feeling of the town. I carry on looking out the window now we are nearly there, as I don't want to miss a thing.

I'm living my dream as the taxi goes through the town. I can't keep the huge smile off my face, and I press against the window like an overexcited child. There are lights strung everywhere, with red ribbon and garlands strung around all the posts and shop fronts. The town is full of decorations, Christmas trees and large candy canes. Even large snowmen and nutcrackers are set out at intervals. I'm itching to get out and look around, but I compose myself. There will be plenty of time for that, I need to go to the inn first. There are small wooden huts being set up for the annual Christmas market that is set to take place in a few days' time, which I can't wait for. There is a huge tree set up in the town square awaiting the tree lighting ceremony; it looks spectacular, can't wait to see it lit up. The town looks just like I hoped it would, and then some, it feels like I've entered a magical Christmas land.

#

Arriving at the inn, I'm completely speechless. It is everything I dreamed it would be, and the picture online really didn't do it justice. Mistletoe Inn is sitting in a huge plot of land and is a white wooden lodge with steps leading to an expansive porch that looks like it wraps all the way around. Just like you see on TV. On the porch is a swing seat with red cushions and blankets. I will use that, most definitely. There is also a seating area in one of the corners that also has blankets in a basket next to it. It looks like a nice place to chill.

I can see myself sitting there reading or with a mug of hot chocolate.

There are two huge Christmas trees on either side of the steps. Red ribbon is wrapped around the posts and the handrails. All the windows have lights and garlands around them. It looks really festive. I take a moment to appreciate my home for the next three weeks. Taking in some deep breaths, I can smell the pine, earthy tones and added to that is a hint of gingerbread; someone must be baking. With that, my tummy gives a little rumble. Standing looking at this gorgeous place, I'm not feeling as cold as I did when I got off the plane. Pulling my cases behind me, I head on inside and am greeted with the warmth and a friendly looking lady placing a plate of gingerbread men on the reception desk. Guess I was right about the baking; they smell and look delicious.

The inside is just as beautiful as the outside. There are garlands around the doorframes with lights around them and poinsettias doted around. There is a tree in what looks like the living room and a log fire that looks very inviting, with high back chairs sitting in front of it. Can't wait to curl up there; it's the ideal place for reading. The dining room on the opposite end also has a tree in one corner. There is a big table in the middle and a few small ones around the outside. Each table has a red tablecloth with either a miniature Christmas tree or a small poinsettia in the middle. The reception desk is small but perfectly adequate; it looks like a lovely inn and has a homely feel to it. I take off my hat, gloves, scarf and undo my coat, then head towards the desk. The lady has a lovely smile on her face.

"Hello, welcome to Mistletoe Inn. My name is Holly."

"Hello Holly, my name is Emma."

"I'll just get you checked in, help yourself to a gingerbread man," and she sets about typing on her computer.

"Thank you. I'll take one to my room with me," I say with a smile while picking a biscuit and wrapping it in a napkin from the side of them.

"Here is your key. You are on the second floor, room 10. I see you are with us three weeks."

"Yes, I'm looking forward to enjoying an American Christmas. It's been a dream of mine to be able to come to a town like this," the excitement evident in my voice.

"There are four more rooms that will be with us for Christmas Day and into the new year, so you won't be on your own. We have activities here at the inn, and in the town. You can sign up for as many or as few as you like. Here is the list of what's going on in town and when, and here is the list of what's going on in here. All I ask is that you give me a heads-up for activities you are joining in here, so I have enough things for everyone," Holly says, handing me two pieces of paper.

"Thank you. I will look through them and let you know. I'm hoping to join in as much as I can." I'm so glad to have a list of the activities that are available. This will help me plan my time efficiently. You got to love a good list to stay organised.

"You're down for breakfast every day. That will be served in the dining room between 7 am and 10 am. You are free to bring in your own food if you want to. Feel free to spend as much time as you like down here in our communal areas. Lastly, the front door will be locked from 11 pm until 6:30 am. This key here is for the front door, and that one is your room key."

18

"Thank you."

"It's a lot to take in, I know, but I'm always around if you need anything. I'll give you a hand with your bags and let you settle in." Thankful for the help, I let her carry a couple of bags. I pick my gingerbread man up and follow her to my room.

#

There is a lovely wooden staircase with open steps that has a super-soft red carpet on to muffle the sound of footsteps. Once at the door to my room, Holly leaves me to it. Inside the room, I take a good look around and I'm delighted with what I see. It is everything I hoped it would be. It is a good-sized room with a double bed in the middle, two bedside tables and a set of drawers. The en-suite is spacious, too, with a large shower and a bath. The size of the room amazes me, as I've never stayed in a room where you can freely move around without minding the furniture. The phrase of being able to swing a cat comes to mind. There is also a table and chair set perfectly in the window. I can see myself sitting there, just enjoying the wonderful view of the rolling hills and distant snow-capped mountains.

The bed has a Christmas duvet on it, which looks inviting. There are fairy lights around the window and a small tree in the corner, perfect for those who bring presents with them. The room feels cosy and smells sweet, but I can't quite place the smell. I know it's familiar, but it's not coming to me yet. Then I notice that there is a diffuser on the dresser and after reading the label telling me its candy cane scent, it becomes obvious to me, see I knew I knew that smell, it definitely adds to the cosy feeling of the room.

After looking around, I sit at the table to eat the delicious gingerbread man. After polishing that off, I then set about emptying my cases, finding room for everything and giving the room a lived-in feel. Then I decide to sit on the bed to see how comfy it is, and I'm pleasantly surprised at how luxurious it feels. I then sit at the table and look at the two flyers' that Holly gave me and work out my schedule. It takes me a minute to get my head around the dates as they write them differently to us, with the month first followed by the day.

I tick the activities that I will be joining in at the inn, which include cookie decorating, ornament decorating, mulled wine and song evening. These are the ones that I definitely want to join in with. In town, there is a gingerbread house decorating competition, snowman competition, weather depending, the tree light switch on is tomorrow night and the market starts the day after. On the 20th is the parade, which takes place in the middle of the town. I'm looking forward to seeing it all and taking part. I put the events on my phone calendar so that I don't miss any. With the jetlag that I'm bound to feel, it could be a possibility of missing something. I am most definitely going to enjoy my time away, and there is lots to do to keep me busy. First, though, I'm going to lie down for a bit and then I will go and explore the town.

#

I wake up a couple of hours later. The jetlag is starting to creep in. I'm feeling hungry, so I set off to find a café. After getting directions from Holly, I head out, and I'm hit by a blast of cold air as I open the door, reminding me just how cold it is here.

It's not a long walk from the inn to the town, which is good for my feet, and the café is easy to find just like Holly said it would be. I can't help but laugh when I read the name of the cafe, Kringle Café, keeping with the Christmas theme of the town, I love it. Inside is like a winter wonderland; there are wooden tables and chairs with Christmas decorations as centre pieces, and red tablecloths cover the tables. The whole place looks very appealing and smells divine.

After placing my order, I send my mum a message, letting her know that I have arrived safe and settled in. I also send her the pictures I took of the inn; I will try calling her tomorrow once I have gotten my head around the time difference. While waiting for my food, I can't help but look around at the wonderful decorations that surround me. It has a homely feel to the place, which leaves me feeling OK about the fact that I'm on my own.

After finishing the most amazing burger, I decide to go for a walk before going back to the inn and to bed. I need to get into the routine of the time zone here. Putting my coat on, I bump into someone with one of my arms. Feeling embarrassed, I turn around to apologise and look at the person I bumped. It turns out I bumped into a very handsome guy. He's tall, muscular and hot. I'm sure I'm starring.

"Sorry about that," I say, knowing that my face is bright red.

"No worries, no harm done," the man replied with a gorgeous smile.

I'm so embarrassed that I hurry out of there, and I'm relieved for the coldness for the first time. I'm mortified to be so clumsy, especially around a guy like that, who probably cursing me as I walked out.

#

Chapter Three

The next morning, I wake to the alarm that I set myself so that I wouldn't oversleep and miss anything. I'm still feeling tired, but I need to acclimatise to the time difference. I cannot succumb to the jetlag. After a most fantastic breakfast of pancakes and maple syrup with bacon, well, I am on holiday. I go back to my room for my coat. I'm off to explore the town properly, as I didn't see much yesterday when I went for food. I'm in such a rush to explore that I go down the stairs as fast as I can, and I end up bumping into someone again. This is becoming a habit, and I'm not normally this clumsy. To my horror, it's the man from last night that makes me even more embarrassed. What must he think of me.

"Sorry," I say while my face goes red, again.

"We meet again," says the man with a gorgeous smile on his face.

"You two have met?" asks Holly curiously, as she is standing with the man.

"I bumped into him last night at Kringle café" I explain.

"My name's Hunter. Holly here is my aunt," Hunter says while winking cheekily at his auntie; it's adorable that he looks at his auntie that way.

"Emma, nice to meet you," I say while holding out my hand for Hunter to shake, which he does and the feel of his hand in mine sends tingles up my arm. I shake my head, trying not to think anything to it.

"Are you going into town? I can give you lift if you like," offers Hunter.

I hesitate to answer, looking awkwardly from Hunter to Holly. I'm not sure what to say. Holly answers for me, sensing my unease.

"It's no bother. He's going into town, and I swear he doesn't bite."

"OK, that would be great, if you're sure you don't mind," I say, looking at Hunter.

Hunter's car is a black pickup, just like the ones you see in the films in towns like this. I get in as gracefully as can. It's higher than anything I have been in before, and what imagined these trucks to be, everyone gets in so easily on the TV. We start off in silence, so I take this time to take Hunter in without making it obvious. He is tall with a muscular body, which I could tell last night, dark brown hair and very kissable looking lips. I quickly look away at this thought. I am not here for a holiday romance, not that I think he likes me but she I need to get my thoughts in order. He really is handsome though, and I can't help turning for another look at him.

"Have you been here long?" Hunter asks, breaking the silence.

"No, got here yesterday."

"How long are you staying?"

"Until 2nd January." We carry on in silence for a couple of minutes as we enter town.

"Is it OK to drop you by the café? I'm going on to the cash and carry for my aunt," asks Hunter.

"Yes, that's fine. Thank you," I say with a smile.

After watching Hunter's truck disappear, I have no idea why I felt the need to stand there watching his car. I take in my surroundings and pick a direction to go in. Both sides of the street are full of shops with more business down the side streets and lots to go and see. The backdrop of the town is full of snow-covered mountains and trees, which make you feel like you are cut off from everywhere. It's a wonderful feeling. Some might find that isolating but not me, as I'm from a small village, not cut off like this but small, this just feels inviting and homely. There is a good variety of shops, which I end up spending the morning looking at and getting the bearings of the town.

After lunch, I head to the bookstore that I spotted earlier. With not bringing any books, expect the one I read on the plane, to help with the weight of my cases, I want to go and get myself a book. The open fire at the inn is inviting me to sit there curled up with a book. When I get there, I notice that there is a for-sale sign and I wonder why it's for sale as it's busy inside and the town is such a tourist attraction it must do well. Once I'm inside, I take my time looking around. It's a beautiful store and has so much potential for the new owners. I end up picking a festive book and then decide to head off back to the inn as I'm eager to start reading. I haven't got very far before a car horn beeps behind me followed with shouting of my name, and I'm momentarily startled until I realise it's Hunter.

"Didn't mean to scare you. I saw you heading this way and thought you might be heading back to the inn. If you, are I can give you lift if you want?"

"Yes, I am. That would be great thanks." My legs are feeling tired.

"Is it the jetlag catching up with you? You look tired. Not in a bad way," says Hunter backtracking.

"It's OK, I probably look as tired as I feel," I say with a small smile while trying to hide my blushing cheeks. If Hunter notices he doesn't say anything, which I'm grateful for.

We then ride to the inn in silence. Once at the inn, I'm about to say thanks for the lift when Hunter catches me off guard.

"Are you going to the tree lighting tonight?"

"I'm hoping to, yeah. Thought I would have a nap, then get some food before going. Are you going?" I ask out of politeness and curiously because I wouldn't mind bumping into him again.

"I am. Would you like me to come and pick you up? Maybe we could eat together beforehand? If you want some company that is," Hunter suggests casually.

"It would be nice to have some company, but don't feel like you have to ask me. I'm OK on my own." I don't want to sound desperate to see him again.

"It would be my pleasure to keep you company. Shall I pick you up at 5?"

"Sounds great." I wave Hunter bye before heading upstairs to my room to drop my stuff off so I can come back down and read for a bit.

#

At four thirty, my alarm goes off after deciding to have a nap to keep myself going for the evening ahead. As I set about getting ready, I feel like I'm getting ready for a date, even though I keep telling myself it's not a date, which doesn't help with my nervousness about the meal. It was nice of Hunter to offer to eat with me and take me to the tree lighting, but I'm

26

not going to read anything into it. We hardly know each other. I'm sure he was just being kind with his offer. Besides, I live in North Wales and that is way too far for a long-distance relationship, plus I don't do flings. I'm not sure why my brain keeps thinking like this, but even though we have only just met, I feel a connection to him. He is easy to be around. After one last look in the mirror to make sure my hair is still straight and neat, I pick up my bag and head downstairs with a smile on my face and a lightness to my walk.

I don't know why I was so nervous. As soon as I saw Hunter, I instantly relaxed. We have just gone to Kringle café, which I don't mind as the food is fantastic. While we are waiting for our food, we talk and laugh as if we have known each other for years. I've never felt a connection like this with a guy before, and it's kind of scary. I learn that Hunter is between jobs after returning home from New York, where he worked in advertising. He was spending the Christmas season helping out his aunt before he decided what he was going to do for work. He says he has an idea of what that will be, but it's too early to tell anyone about it. We talk about our mutual love of books, which we have both read, liked and disliked. We come to realise that we actually have a lot in common. While we are on the topic of books, I ask if he knows why the bookshop is for sale. It's a lovely shop and would be a great business to own. I can see the potential that it has.

"The current owners can't handle the workload anymore. I'm hoping whoever buys it keeps it as bookstore; it's the only one we have here in the town." Explains Hunter, I notice a twinkle in his eyes while talking about it. It must be special to him.

"It would be a shame if it couldn't be kept as bookstore. There is nothing like being surrounded by books. You don't get the smell or texture from an e-book; I'd much rather have a physical book any day."

"I know what you mean. I'm more a book person than e-book, although they do have their advantages."

"They do. I'll give you that. It must be nice to own a bookstore. You don't get many independent ones near me. There are far too many commercial ones."

"That is a shame. There is no soul in these big commercial stores," Hunter replies, and I notice the twinkle in his eyes again. I wonder if this is the idea that's too early to talk about. I guess I will have to see if he tells me at any point. Good luck to him if he is trying to buy it.

"We had best get going if you want to see the lights switched on," he says while looking at his watch, a quick change of subject, but after looking at the time myself, I realise how long we have been here for, and we do indeed need to get going.

#

Outside, the temperature has dropped quite a bit as we make our way to the town square. Hunter leaves the car where it is, as it's a short distance to the town square. We arrive just in time to start the count down with everyone. I'm so glad I didn't miss it even though I was enjoying talking to Hunter. It is a big crowd that has turned up, bigger than I expected, and it makes me feel like part of the community. No one is left standing separately; the locals have accepted everyone as one of them. It's a wonderful atmosphere to be a part of, and it helps to take the chill off with the warm feeling it gives you being surrounded by so much generosity. The tree smells wonderful, mixed with the crisp air and the mix of hot drinks that people are holding to keep their hands warm. Everyone cheers at the end of the countdown, which adds to the atmosphere.

Once the lights are on, I look around in awe. The tree is beautiful, its tall, wide and full, with white lights and a glowing star on top. It is the biggest Christmas tree that I have ever seen. It must have taken days to put up all those lights, plus a very tall ladder for the star, if such a thing exists. Maybe they used the fire truck; that makes sense. I'm glad I don't seem to be the only one who is looking at the tree in awe. I don't feel like I stand out.

I then wander towards the wooden gazebo, which is to the side, set back a bit. It is covered in white lights and has red ribbon weaved around the structure. It looks beautiful and seems like the ideal place to sit and take everything in, or just to be with your own thoughts. I can see myself spending some time here, both at night and in the day. The pathway leading up to it is lit up with giant candy canes, adding to the Christmas vibe. One might think it's over the top, but it just fits right in with the rest of the town. I'm busy taking pictures with my phone when Hunter offers to take a picture of me with the tree and gazebo in the background. I'm delighted, as this is a great opportunity to show my mum how happy I am here. After posing for a few pictures, I manage to persuade Hunter to take a selfie with me in front of the tree.

Just then, it starts to snow and the smile on my face gets bigger and bigger. While I'm looking up at the snow falling with my arms spread out and turning in circles, I can feel

Hunter watching me. He seems mesmerised at how happy I am with a few snowflakes. It's all normal to him. He probably thinks I'm mad, but I don't get to see much snow and it's the icing on the cake for a beautiful night.

Half an hour of enjoying the snow, Hunter puts his arm around my shoulders and his arm feels nice around me, so I step a bit closer to him, now that I've noticed how cold I am. We don't say anything to each other; we just share a look with one another and walk back to his truck. Hunter keeps his arm around me; we both have big smiles on our faces. Having his arm around me felt natural, and I immediately felt cold when we got into the car. The closeness made butterflies flutter in my tummy. It's a wonderful feeling and one I haven't felt before.

"Thank you for tonight. I had a great time," I say as Hunter pulls up outside the inn, now that a bit of time has passed, I feel slightly conscious of having his arm around me, so I quickly say bye so that I'm not that close to him any longer.

"It was my pleasure. I hope to see you around," Hunter replies with the smile on his face. That smile is so disarming. I just melt every time I see it.

With that thought, I head to my room and send some pictures of the tree and the snow falling to Mum. I will try calling her tomorrow, as it is proving hard to get my head around the time difference. I lay in bed reflecting on the fantastic day that I've had, and I can't wait to see and do and more, plus to see more of Hunter.

#

Chapter Four

The following morning, I wake up looking forward to seeing the market. A wonderful sight meets me when I open the inn door. There is a thick blanket of snow everywhere; it is beautiful. Apparently, this is light snowfall, according to Holly, but to me this is more snow than I have seen before. It crunches under my feet as I walk around the inn, enjoying the feel of it under my feet. I don't even notice the cold that much. With not many footprints in the snow, I set about making my own, making sure to only walk where no one else has this morning. Until I get to town and where the market is, there is hardly any untouched snow, and my mood dips a little at this, but then I look up at the stalls and my mood is restored. The gritters have been out so the roads are clear, and the paths aren't too slippery either, which is good. I wouldn't want to slip and get an injury that would definitely put a damper on things.

The market looks amazing, all set up of wooden chalets which are dotted around the town square and open areas of the main shopping street. They all have lights on them and are decorated with Christmas decorations. They suit the town blending in with everything. It's like they belong there. The smells coming from the market stalls is amazing. I'm walking around taking in deep breaths, smelling everything from hot chocolate to citrus and pine. It smells just like Christmas should.

I start off getting myself a hot chocolate to drink while walking around to help keep my hands warm so I can get a feel of the stalls available. There are stalls with a wide range of foods, homemade wreaths, decorations both homemade and manufactured, drinks of surprising flavours, both hot and cold and bottled to give as gifts, and the most incredible handmade jewellery I have ever seen. Everything looks so tantalising, and with most things being handmade, it's hard not to buy everything that I want to. This is going to be a great exercise in self-control; I only have so much weight left in my luggage allowance. At a stall selling handmade wooden tree ornaments, I can't resist buying a couple to take home with me; they are so beautifully made. I pick one of Santa on a one-horse open sleigh and one of a cute snowmen. I might even put them on the tree in my room back at the inn.

An hour later, and I'm still looking around the market when I spot Hunter talking to some people. I don't want to bother him as he looks deep in conversation, so I carry on walking around trying not to make it obvious that I have spotted him. I don't want him to think that he is obliged to talk to me after last night. The next moment, though, Hunter is briskly walking towards me.

"Hi. Thought that was you I saw."

"Hi. Yea, sorry, I didn't want to come and say hi, you looked busy."

"No problem," says Hunter as he matches his stride to mine. "What do you think to our little market?"

"It's amazing, but I wouldn't call it little. There are so many talented people out here. I've picked up a couple of things, trying not to buy everything I want, or I won't have room to take it home," I say while showing Hunter my bag of goodies and laughing.

"Yes, that could be a problem," he says while trying to stifle a giggle.

"I was just about to head to Kringle Café to warm up a bit. Fancy joining me for a coffee?" I hope I don't sound too hopeful; I don't want to come across as needy or that I have any exceptions after last night.

"Sorry, I can't. I've got somethings I need to do for my aunt. Next time, though," Hunter says rather apologetically.

"No problem." I'm hoping that I don't look disappointed; it's not like we have known each other long. I can't help it, though; I do feel a tang of disappointment.

I head off to Kringle Café for some lunch and then decide to walk around the market again to soak up the atmosphere. It's a lovely atmosphere with people chatting and music playing; they are shoppers everywhere. This is what I wanted to experience, and I'm loving every second of it. So far, the place is living up to my dreams, and I'm so glad I came.

#

While on my second look around the market, I notice that there is a stall where you can make your wreath. They have a separate table for making, which is filled with everything you could want to decorate a wreath. The ones that they are selling are spectacular. It looks like a lot of fun, so I decide to have a go. I haven't made one before, so I'm not holding out much hope for the end product, but I will enjoy myself, nevertheless.

From the huge variety of items to choose from, I decide to start with wrapping some of the thick red ribbon around it and adding a bow at the bottom. It's not the best bow, but it will do. Then I add some sprigs of holly and some cinnamon sticks that are three wrapped together to add to the aroma so it is starting to smell divine. For a finishing touch, I add some poinsettias here and there and a sprinkle of glitter. I'm very happy with my finished product; it has turned out much better than I thought it would. I also buy an over-the-door hanger for it with the hope of adding it to my room's door. I'm sure Holly won't mind. Plus, it would be great to take a picture of it hanging up to send back home.

#

Back at the inn, I can't wait to show off my wreath to Holly. I've had a huge smile on my face carrying it back with me. I'm feeling proud of my accomplishment.

"Holly, do you mind if I hang this on my door? I've just made it at the market." Once, I've located her in the office.

"Wow, that is beautiful, Emma, of course you can," Holly replies, admiring my handiwork, which adds to my smile. It's always nice to know that other people like something that you have made.

Once I've hung up the wreath, I decided to take the book I was reading this morning and sit in the lounge in front of the fire to continue reading. It's a great spot, with the high back chair and the fire warms me up nicely. Plus, I love the smell of an open fire. You don't get many open fireplaces in my area of Wales—not ones that get used anyway.

While sitting there, I meet a couple of the guests with whom I will be spending Christmas day.

"Have you been coming here a while?" I ask the young family.

"Six years. We used to go to the big bed and breakfast up the road, but when Holly opened up here four years ago, we thought we'd try here for a change. It's closer to town and it's a more homely feel here. Holly is big part of that. She is always adding to the activities that she puts on; the kids love it."

"Holly has done a wonderful job with this place. I agree that she makes it feel like home away from home."

"Do you think you will be back here?"

"I've love to, and hopefully one day I will be."

It is good to be able to chat with the other guests and get advice from them on where to go and what to see. They tell me about the skiing and sledding, which I hadn't even thought of. Of course, there are slopes nearby. If I get a chance, I will check it out.

Holly then comes around offering out hot chocolate and homemade cookies to her guest. This is something she does every afternoon, so I make a mental note to be here as much as I can at this time to be able to mingle with everyone. Everyone is friendly and welcoming that I don't feel like I'm away on my own. There is always someone who is willing to involve you in their activities, but they respect your alone time too.

#

Chapter Five

Today is the gingerbread house decorating competition in town. I've been looking forward to this, to see the creations of my fellow competitors, and to give it a try myself. I head to the town hall, where it is taking place, and I bump into the family I met yesterday. They offer to split their team, so I'm not on my own, but I'm happy to be a team of one. Besides, I don't want to split the family up, even though they offered, as it is one of their traditions, they take part in the event every year. Plus, I'm looking forward to seeing what I can make on my own, as I've given it a lot of thought.

Inside rows of tables have been set up with the house pieces in a pile at each with bags of icing sugar for each team. In the middle of the tables are bowls full of different sweets for decorating. It looks like it is going to be fun, and it smells sweet and spicy from the gingerbread. The sweets look very tempting to dip into and will make the houses pop with colour. I will just have to not eat them before I've built my house.

At the other end of the hall, I can see that there are tables set out for the more experienced builder, where they are bringing their own gingerbread and decorations and creating whatever they like. This is where all the big extravagant buildings are made, like the ones you see in films and TV. They have their own competition too with ribbons for the top three, whereas the one I'm joining in with is more for fun, there is still first, second and third place up for grabs though.

At the end, we get to take the houses home with us, which is a win for everyone, I think.

There is Christmas music playing quietly in the background, mixing with the sounds of laughter and talking; the atmosphere is great. I find a place at the table, then we are given half an hour to construct our houses and to decorate them. It doesn't sound like long, but that is where the fun is. See what you can do in a short space of time. It does make it a bit chaotic but so much fun as well.

It takes me a while to get mine to stand on its own. The roof keeps sliding off, which then makes the sides topple, but I get there in the end. I have done my best with the piping in the time given; it isn't great and it's a lot harder to do than it looks, especially in a hurry. I then stick loads of different size sweets onto it to try and hide the blemishes and to add decorations like windows and a door. When the bell rings to signify the end, I look up and down the table and back to my creation, and I can't help but laugh at the mess that is my house. Most of the others look like pros at this, but it's the taking part that counts, and I've had loads of fun doing just that. I'm under no illusions that I'm going to win, or come third for that matter, but in the end, I have a yummy gingerbread house to take back to the inn with me.

#

Once the judging is finished, with lots of cheering for the winners, I pick up my house, thankful for the box I have been given to carry it in. Also, this way, no one could see it, so I feel happy to go and see how the professionals are getting on at the end of the hall. I'm amazed at what I see; someone is making Santa's workshop, another is making a clock tower and one group is even making a Ferris wheel which moves, how amazing is that. They are all looking spectacular. I don't envy the judges when it comes time for them to make their decision.

I decide to stay and see how they all turn out, amazed at the techniques that are being used. An hour later and the results are in, Santa's workshop wins and the round of applause that they receive is fantastic; these must have been the favourite. After joining in the congratulations, I decide to head back to the inn. When I get back, Holly is waiting to see how I did and how the other guests had gotten on.

"It's a bit of a mess, but I enjoyed it," I say while opening the box. I may as well say it myself, so Holly doesn't feel the need to be overly nice.

"It's not that bad, Emma. Do you want to put it on the dining table so everyone can enjoy it?"

"That would be great. Then everyone can help themselves to a piece. I don't think I should eat the whole thing myself. I just need a picture to send back home first," I say, taking my phone out of my bag to take the picture.

"You stand holding it and I'll take a picture for you," Holly offers, and I take her up on it as it will be nice for Mum to see me in some pictures having a good time.

"Thanks, Holly. It would be good to get one with me in it."

#

Pictures taken, I thank Holly before heading to my room to give Mum a call.

"Darling, how are you? The pictures you have sent look fab."

"Hi, Mum. I'm so happy; it's amazing here. The gingerbread house competition was so much fun. I think I need more practice though," I say while laughing.

"Maybe just a bit." My mum joins in with me laughing.

"It's just how I imagined it to be here. Colder than you think, though. I'm so glad I came." I want to reassure Mum that I'm doing OK, and that she doesn't need to worry about me.

"You're not too lonely, are you?"

"No, well, maybe sometimes, but I'm OK. Everyone I have met is really nice. Holly, the owner, always asks how I am and if I need anything. Her nephew is nice, too. We have been out for food, and he walked me to the tree lighting the other night. He seems really nice. We got on like a house on fire, and he is good looking too."

"As long as you're happy. Be careful with this man though, you hardly know him, and you are in a strange country," Mum says in her warning tone.

"I'm being careful, Mum. I'm going to go; I'll try and call soon."

"OK, love, you take care of yourself. Keep sending photos. Speak to you soon."

We say our goodbyes, then I go downstairs to have a piece of my house. When I get in the dining room, there are more guests there enjoying the gingerbread and chatting away to each other. I spend the rest of the evening soaking up the atmosphere and getting to know my fellow guests.

#

Chapter Six

I start the day with a walk and a lite lunch at Kringle Cafe before heading back to the inn ready for the ornament-making session that Holly has planned for this afternoon. This is one of the activities that I've been looking forward to, as I enjoy making things. I haven't seen Hunter since the market, and I am surprised to see him at the table looking ready to join in. With excited anticipation of seeing Hunter again, I quickly take my coat and bag upstairs and check out my reflection before heading back down to the dining room.

Hunter is no longer standing there, and I feel a stab of sadness that I quickly shake off, not knowing where that came from. Then, I sit at the table looking at the supplies and wondering what there is to make and coming up with ideas. There are paint pens, stencils, stickers, glitter, wooden-shaped tree ornaments and cards. There is definitely something for everybody here. Just then Hunter is back with a tray of hot chocolates and Holly is behind him with some cookies, fresh from the oven, and they smell amazing like normal.

"Everybody help yourselves to a drink and cookies. As you can see, there are lots of things available to make, help yourselves, and not just to one thing, to anything you like. Have fun!" says Holly, smiling at us all.

With that, everyone descends to the middle of the table, so I take this opportunity to get myself a drink first and a delicious cookie, of course. I have just picked up a couple of tree decorations and some paint pens when Hunter takes a seat next to me, setting those darn butterflies off again.

"Are you having a good time here in our little town?"

"I am, yes. I've been going for walks, enjoying the snow. We don't get much where I'm from. I joined in the gingerbread house competition yesterday; that was fun. Tomorrow, I'm going to take part in the snowman competition. Do you take part in any of the activities in town?" I can't help asking, curious about his answer.

"I did when I was younger. Maybe I will again. Do you have a partner for tomorrow? It will be hard work on your own."

"I don't, no, but I'm not scared of hard work," I say a bit defensively.

"I can see that about you, but I didn't mean it in a bad way. Just that rolling that much snow is tough," Hunter replies, holding his hands up.

"You could always come and help me," I say jokingly.

After a moment of silence, Hunter says, "OK, you're on," and we shake hands on it.

"What about now? Are you going to make or decorate something?" I ask, indicating at the table.

"Why not, Looks like fun. Plus, the company isn't too bad," Hunter says, nudging my arm.

We spend the next couple of hours at the table, decorating and chatting. I don't even realise that we are the last two people still here. Holly has just brought us more drinks as we continue discussing our lives. It's easy conversation, and we just bounce of each other.

"What's your favourite thing about Christmas?" Hunter asks me.

"That's a hard question. Everything." I start to giggle.

"There must be something," Hunter says, laughing with me.

"I suppose it's the atmosphere. How happy people tend to be this time of year."

"There is a certain jolliness to this season."

"How about you? What's your favourite bit?"

"This place. Don't get me wrong. New York was always great, but nowhere does Christmas like we do here."

"What made you decide to leave New York?"

"I never really adjusted to city life. When my job came to an end, I thought it was life telling me to go back home."

"So, you believe in destiny and fate?"

"I wouldn't say I'm a big believer, but I was missing home, then I got made redundant. It kind of gave me the push I needed."

"What made you move out there in the first place?"

"A few things. I wanted to see more of America, and going off to uni gave be the bug to move. I also got a great job opportunity." I can sense that there is more to it, but I won't push.

"Look at the time. I'd best get going. I've taken up too much of your time, as it is," says Hunter, after looking at his watch.

"I've enjoyed talking to you. You haven't taken up any time."

"Still want to spend the morning together building a snowman tomorrow, or have you had enough of me?"

"Not sick of you, and yes, to help. If you still want to, that is?"

"I'll meet you here in the morning and walk you to the competition. Don't forget your gloves," Hunter says with a wink.

"See you tomorrow."

I watch Hunter leave before collecting my makes, but as I'm about to go upstairs, I have an idea, so I sit back down. I want to make Hunter a card to say thank you for making me feel so welcome. Taking my time to make sure it's perfect, I'm hoping he likes it. I can't believe how well we get on, and I feel like I could really fall for him. I am feeling happier than I have in ages, and I know part of that is because of Hunter. It's also being here, the place I have dreamed of coming to for so long. It feels like home, and I have often thought about living in America but never thought that I actually would. Not that I'm thinking of moving out here, but my mind keeps wondering what it would be like, especially when I'm around Hunter or thinking about him. I have some soul searching to do.

#

Chapter Seven

I wake the next morning to the sight of a fresh blanket of snowfall and a wave of excitement washes over me about the day ahead. It has been a long time since I built a snowman. Living in North Wales, I haven't seen much snow and nowhere on the scale that it is here. Here you can see the snow as far as your eyes can see, and it looks spectacular, like someone has put a white blanket over everything.

I decide to wait outside for Hunter. While I'm waiting, I look around to see if there is anyone around, then I decide to make a snow angel. It always looks so much fun in the films, but I didn't particularly want anyone to see me. Before I can get up, though, I see Hunter looking at me trying to stifle a laugh, so I gather up a ball of snow and throw it at him. I manage to catch him on the arm. I jump up just as he throws a snowball at me, so I quickly duck out the way. After a couple of minutes of throwing snowballs at each other, we call a truce and head to the snowman competition laughing.

I notice that Hunter is carrying a bag. "What's in the bag?"

"Supplies. We want to win, don't we?" Hunter replies winking at me, which gives me goose bumps all over.

When we get there, I notice that there are 10 groups taking part, including two groups from the inn. We get fifteen minutes to build our snowman, and there is just the winning team, no second or third. This is fine with me, as I just want to take part, but I think Hunter wants to win judging by his body language. He takes charge and tells me to make the head while he makes the body. We both get on with our tasks, then Hunter lifts the head into place and starts packing snow around the joins. After Hunter is happy with how it looks, he opens the bag he brought with him and takes out two large pinecones, which he tells me to use as ears. He has stones for eyes and a mini carrot for a nose. Next, he says, is his secret weapon, a green Christmas waist coat and an elf hat. I step back, allowing him to finish the snowman off as he clearly has a vision and admires his precision for the task. For a finishing touch, he adds a wooden toy train, making it look like the elf is holding it. What a genius idea. It looks great, and we finish just in time.

"I can't believe you had all this stuff; it looks fantastic," I say excitedly, hoping we have a chance at winning.

"It's stuff I had from a kid. I did this the last time I took part but didn't win. That's why I've added the train. Hopefully it will give us the edge." Hunter is beaming at me. I can tell he wants to be able to finally win.

I can't believe we won. I scream with joy and hug Hunter when the judges announce that we won with our elf. My cheek brushes against his and I can feel his breath warming me; it's intoxicating. We stay like that for a moment longer than necessary, and then we both pull away at the same time with awkward looks on our faces. Neither of us knows what to do next. Hunter then explains that they keep the snowmen dressed up for a couple of days, and then everyone is free to take back their belongings. It gives everyone a chance to admire them. It's a sweet idea, and the snowmen do look better all dressed up. It's nice to be able to admire them all.

#

We walk around for a bit before heading back to the inn, and for the first time, there is an uncomfortable silence between us. To break it and get back to how we normally are around each other, I decide to start another snowball fight and instantly the playful Hunter is back.

While running around dodging balls as well as throwing them, we end up sprawled on the ground, laughing. Seeing as I was on the floor, I decide to do another snow angel and encourage Hunter to do one with me. He hesitates at first but is soon joining me in making an angel. Hunter gets up first and offers his hands to help me up. He pulls a bit too hard, and I end up with my face right in front of him, both of us steading our breathing. He smells divine with his citrus shampoo and the pine scent emitting from him. Hunter then gently brushes his lips against mine. My stomach is doing somersaults. He then gently nudges my lips open and slides his tongue against mine. I'm immediately pulled into the heat of the kiss, need coming from both of us. I have never been kissed like this before. My knees start to feel weak. By the time we pull apart, we are both breathless, and I'm all shaky. Hunter puts his arm around my waist and we carry on walking. I'm instantly relaxed with his arm there, my shakes under control, walking like this feels natural, and I know then that I'm in big trouble here. I'm lost in thought when Hunter turns to look at me.

"I know we need to discuss the kiss, which was amazing by the way, but can it wait till later?"

"There's no rush, and yea, it was great," I say the last bit in a whispered tone. We then kiss again before continuing on our way. It wasn't as hot and needy as the first kiss, but it was still amazing.

#

"What are you doing for food later? Do you want to go out with me and get something?" Hunter asks once we are back at the inn.

"I'd love to go out with you."

"Great. I'll pick you up about six. Oh, and wear something nice as I'm going to take you somewhere nice," Hunter says before he kisses me goodbye.

I am so happy I can't stop smiling as I dreamily make my way to my room. I keep thinking that if we didn't live so far apart, it could become something. The fact is, though, that the distance is there, but I have never felt like this, and I don't do flings. I also know that this is more than a holiday romance. Hunter is right; we do need to talk.

Later on, I get changed into one of the dresses I brought with me and put my hair in an updo. I take my time to make sure I look my best. Hunter is waiting for me when I get downstairs, but he looks to be in a heated conversation with his aunt, so I clear my throat to announce them to my presence. Holly wishes both goodnight and walks off. I can't help but feel like that discussion was about me. I try not to dwell on it during the drive to the restaurant.

I'm glad I picked this dress to wear, as Hunter has chosen an Italian restaurant. It looks romantic with red table clothes and a candle in the middle of each table, soft music playing in the background. Hunter is looking very nice in a dark pair of jeans and a shirt. I can smell his citrus shampoo stronger than before, and his aftershave is fresh, and earthy.

"Was everything OK with your aunt?" I ask once we have ordered. I can't stand it any longer. I need to know.

"Yea, she's just worried about me."

"Because of me?"

"Of us, she doesn't want me to get hurt when you leave. We are getting to know each other, and I don't want to change that, unless you do?"

"No, I'm enjoying getting to know you. We don't know what this is between us, yet. I would like to find out though."

"Yeah, me too," Hunter replies, taking hold of my hand over the table.

The rest of the meal is spent with easy-flowing conversation. Talk eventually turns to my plans for the next few days, leading up to Christmas. I have two things left that I want to do and that is ice skating and watching the Christmas parade in a couple of days' time. I'm also joining in the cookie decorating afternoon at the inn the day after tomorrow.

"I've been wanting to ask, why here for Christmas and not New York, say?" Hunter asks me.

"New York would be nice, but only for a few days. I love Christmas and all films Christmas; they make it all so magical. You get the snow here, the community spirit, a cute inn. Films and books inspired me, but when I searched for somewhere, I couldn't resist coming to a town called Mistletoe. I wanted to be able to join in with things. My mum thought I was mad coming on my own, but with being made redundant, it seemed like fate. When else would I be able to go away for three weeks. America has always appealed to me, but I just had to see it at Christmas."

"I can understand your mum's concerns. I'm glad you came and not just because I like you but for you, you've got to do what is right for you. How are we living up to the films and books?"

"Pretty good, actually. These past six days have been so much fun. I love this town, it feels homely, and everyone has been really welcoming."

"Have you ever thought about moving out here?"

"I have, but never actually looked into it. How about you? Ever thought about moving to another country?"

"Honestly, no. I've lived in New York, but I feel at home here. I believe this is where I belong." He wants to be honest with me, and I admire that.

"Have you thought about what you are going to do in the new year for work?" I ask, wanting to change the subject from moving.

"Actually, yea. I'm trying to buy the bookshop," Hunter says with a hopeful tone.

"That's amazing. I'd love to own one, and that one has so much potential." I'm happy for him.

"My thoughts exactly. What would you do with it, then?" Hunter asks.

"Well, I'd change the name and add a slogan. Mistletoe Books, fall in love with reading, or something like that. I'd put a sofa and a couple of chairs in the window area to create a relaxed atmosphere and allow people to enjoy a book surrounded by books. You could add a beanbag section for a reading area for the children," I reply enthusiastically.

"You have put some thought into it. I like your seating idea; I might have to use it."

"Please do. You could add mistletoe cushions to carry the name inside too," I add as the thought pops into my mind.

We continue exchanging ideas for a while before we realise how late it is. We make plans to go ice skating tomorrow afternoon. I'll be glad for the company, as it has been a long time since I last skated, so having an arm to lean on will be great reassurance. Plus, the company is great, and I am really enjoying getting to know Hunter.

#

Chapter Eight

The next day, I decide to spend the morning researching how to move to America, with work visas and green cards. I'm curious to know how easy it would be to live here. An idea came to me last night that I could move for a year to give me the chance to see if I could make the move permanent and be this far from my family. I also do a search for local jobs in this area, as I love it here so much, and to see what opportunities there are here for an event planner. I am looking for a job, after all. Then there is Hunter. He is big factor for this research, but I don't want to uproot for a fleeting romance. What if it didn't work out, I would be a long way from home with no family or friends.

After a good couple of hours of research, all I have worked out is that it can take a while to get a work visa, plus I would have to be somewhere else to get a job in my field. I would also need a place to live, which is a task on its own. This was all hypothetical, though, as I just wanted to know how it would work. It is a dream I have had for a long time and now that I'm in America, the dream is more prominent. Also, if I were to do it, now would be a good time, as I don't have a job and I'm single. My mind is a whirl of thoughts and ideas that I wasn't expecting to have. I give myself a good talk to, to enjoy my holiday and get myself ready to go for lunch.

After lunch, I make my way to the ice-skating rink at the park to meet Hunter. It's a basic rink, but with the trees and lights, it feels cosy. I'm early, so I decide to get a hot chocolate from the nearby stand, which is perfectly placed near the rink entrance, and then find a bench to sit on and people watch. The air is crisp and filled with laughter from the families, couples, who are skating and the passer-bye. It's a wonderful site and makes me feel happy to be able to witness such joy and carefreeness. I'm lost in thought when Hunter sits down next to me that it takes me a double look to realise it's him.

"Sorry, I was miles away."

"No problem. Are you OK?"

"Yea, just lost in thought. Ready to skate?" I ask while getting up and putting my empty cup in the nearby bin.

Once we have our skates on, Hunter takes my hand to steady me as I get on the ice. I haven't skated for years and I'm a bit wobbly. It takes me a couple of minutes and a couple of near misses to fall on my bottom before I get a rhythm going. We skate around with everyone else and even though I have the hang of it now, I don't let go of Hunter's hand. It feels natural to be there and gives me a warm feeling. Hunter doesn't seem to mind, which makes me feel hopeful that he does seem to like me. From last night's conversation, it would have to be me who moves so that we can have a chance and that is a lot of pressure on me.

I push that thought aside and just concentrate on spending time with him in the here and now. The rink has been set up beautifully, with snowmen and penguins on the ice and trees outside. There is even music playing from the skate hut. It is a relaxed atmosphere with everyone skating by nicely; no one is trying to show off, and everyone is respectful of everyone else.

We have a great time on the ice and end up skating for over an hour before we realise. We then decide to sit and get a drink of hot chocolate. Hunter tells me how he is getting on with buying the bookshop. He looks excited for his new adventure, and he has already started designing his website. At the moment, the shop has no social media presence, so getting that set up is one of the first things he wants to get done. It is vital in this day and age to have a presence online as it helps towards sales as a lot of people shop online. It will also allow him to get a wider audience.

"Your face lights up when you talk about the shop."

"It has been a dream of mine for so long and one that I thought would stay that way, a dream. I feel honoured to have this chance."

"I'm happy for you that you are able to make a dream of yours come true."

"Just like you have done with this trip," Hunter says while nudging my arm.

"Here's to making our dreams come true," I say, holding my hot chocolate up to his.

After finishing our drinks, we decide to go for a walk, and Hunter points out his old hangouts from when he was a child.

"What was it like growing up here?"

"It was great. Winters are always like this, so I learnt to ski. My mates and I would go skiing or sledging most weekends. Summers, we would go swimming in the nearby lake. We were always hiking and cycling, too."

"Sounds like a very active upbringing. I played outside and cycled but not as much as it sounds like you did."

"Not much else to do around here really. I wasn't always out and about, though. Sometimes, I would sit in a field or up a tree and read for hours on end. I didn't really play sports, as I preferred to read or draw. How about you? Did you play many sports?"

"Only what we had to do in PE. I liked helping out with the school events. That's where I started to want to pursue it as a career. I managed to get some work experience with a hotel manager and that sealed my fate. I loved every minute of it."

"I always enjoyed drawing but not to the extent of being an artist. I sort of fell into graphic design while I was at uni."

"Do you still draw?"

"I do, but only for me."

"Have you ever thought of becoming an illustrator? That would combine your skill with what you enjoy."

"You know what, that's what I've been thinking about lately. It would work around the bookstore."

"Have all your school friends moved away?"

"Some have, like the gang I used to hang out with. They come occasionally and we catch up over a beer. There are still some classmates still here, like Lucy, the girl at the counter in Kringles. You tend to find that some moved back home eventually."

It's been nice hearing stories about his youth; it gives me a better understanding of the man that he is. We stop to get hot dogs from a stall at the market and eat them in the gazebo by the big tree.

As we are sitting there, a group of people turn up by the tree and start singing Christmas carols. It's a wonderful sight, as more people join in. I find myself singing along and then getting up to stand with everyone else. I notice that Hunter is still sitting there, but he has his phone out videoing me, so I smile at him and carry-on singing. When the next song starts, Hunter is at my side and he has his arm snaked around my waist and he too starts singing. I love the feel of his arm around me, and I snuggle closer into him. We end up staying until the sing-along is finished and then Hunter walks me back to the inn. It has been a fun day and the impromptu singing session topped it off. I ask Hunter to send me the video he took of me so I can send it to my mum.

"Thanks for this afternoon. It's been wonderful."

"It was my pleasure."

We kiss goodbye, and I go in the inn on a high. I am truly happy to be here, and I don't want it to end.

#

Chapter Nine

Hunter is busy the next day with paperwork for the shop and he is also running errands for his aunt. I'm OK with having the day to myself, as it gives me time to think about the budding feelings that I have for Hunter. The time spent on my own will be good for me. I have the cookie decorating session this afternoon at the inn, so this morning, I go for a walk. I have gotten into a good routine of a morning walk, and it helps to clear my mind and wakes me up, as the morning air is always crisp. The walk will do my weight good, too, with all the extra food I'm eating.

This morning, though, I didn't realise how far I have walked until I see the sign for the tree farm at the edge of the town. Seems that I have gone this far I carry on walking to the farm. It will be nice to look around one even though I don't need a tree. I've not been to a Christmas tree farm before, as we always have a fake tree at home. Everyone around here seems to have a real one and they do smell nice, and they don't all lose their pines like I thought they did.

Once there, I'm greeted by an older gentleman.

"Tie this ribbon on to the tree you would like and then come and get me and I will cut it down for you," he says, holding out a blue ribbon.

"I'm not looking for a tree, but I would like a look around, if that's OK?"

"No problem, lass."

I smile at him my thanks and set off towards the trees. Who knew that there are so many different types. There are signs telling what they are like Douglas fir, Blue spruce and balsam fir. They all smell different and there are various sizes all around. After taking in the smells and the different feel of the trees, I head back to the entrance where there are a few wooden chalets, like the ones in the town. I didn't notice them on my way in, as I was mesmerised by the sheer number of trees. There is one selling wreaths, one selling tree decorations and a couple of food and drink ones.

I end up buying more tree decorations. I can't help myself; they are beautiful. The talent of people never seizes to amaze me. At one of the food stalls, someone is selling handmade fudge, so I get myself some candy cane fudge to eat with a drink before I walk back. It tastes amazing. I end up buying more in different flavours to take back with me.

While I'm on my way back, I decide to have a quick look around the market to see if there are any new stalls or products. I notice a stall selling handmade fabric items and I go and have a look. There are cushions, tablecloths and bunting, all made with Christmas themed fabric. I see a bunting made from red fabric with mistletoe printed on it and decide to get it as a present for Hunter, as it will look great in his new bookshop. I also spot a Santa print fabric that has been made into an apron and I get that for myself. With time running out before the cookie decorating, take my purchases and go back to the inn.

#

In the dining room, the big table is set up ready for cookie decorating. There are piping bags with different coloured icings and tubs of sweets, lots of them. It smells delicious in there with a mixture of icing and sweets. Then there is the smell coming from the kitchen, ginger and chocolate chip cookies. My mouth is watering, just looking and smelling everything. I'm glad of the big walk. I won't feel so guilty eating some of this goodness.

On the table are shortbread biscuits that are ready for icing. Guests are starting to gather now, as Holly comes out with plates of different types of cookies. She sets these down on a different table so that they can cool down before icing. There is another table that looks like it is for decorated cookies to set. On a small table, there are bags of different sizes and ties to be able to tie them up. It all looks very professionally set out and I can't wait to get stuck in.

"Good afternoon, everyone. Thank you for taking part this afternoon. There are lots of cookies to decorate. For those of you who are here for the first time, I would like to tell you why we are decorating all these cookies today. We have one hundred to decorate and bag up and this evening they will be going to the local homeless shelter. This is our way to give back. You don't have to stay until they are all done. You do as many or as little as you like. This is your holiday. We are grateful for any help that we get, so thank you for taking part. There will be cookies left over, so you can eat one or two. Right, let's get decorating!" Holly says with gusto.

I had no idea that was why we are decorating the cookies and I'm glad to be a part of it. It feels good to be able to give back. I did wonder who would eat all the cookies that we are going to make. I'm glad they are going to people who could do with a nice treat.

There is lots of chatter and laughter as the afternoon roles on and everyone is enjoying themselves. It's a lot of fun and I'm enjoying creating different designs. Holly must have been busy baking as the more we decorate, the newer ones seem to appear in the dining room. No one seems to mind, though, as everyone stays until they all done and, in the end, we have one hundred and fifty cookies.

I talk to the couple sitting next to me; it's their first time here too.

"We're from LA, so we don't get any snow. I've seen snow before but not this thick. It's our first Christmas together and we wanted it to be extra special, so we came here. The snow just makes Christmas more magical. It is, however, a lot colder than we are used to." She laughs at this.

"I imagine you're finding it colder than me. Wales gets cold and some light snow but nowhere near like this."

"It deferentially takes a bit of getting used to, but it makes all the difference to the atmosphere of Christmas."

"It sure does. I can't imagine a hot Christmas." That would be my worst Christmas.

"It's really good of Holly and the guests to be doing this. I'm honoured to be a part of it."

"Me too. This isn't what I was expecting when I signed up. I just thought it would be a few cookies for us to be eating, but this is so much better."

"It is. It's nice to know that we will put a smile on other people's faces when they get these."

We then get on with the task of bagging them up and that takes longer than I thought it would, but I didn't mind. Once the last one is bagged, we all help ourselves to cookies and carry on chatting and having fun. Holly brings out wine, beer and juice. It was decided that after all that work, a drink was needed.

"Holly, what made you buy this place and turn it into a bed and breakfast?"

"This house has been sitting empty for years and I could always see the potential in it. I used to work in hotels as a manager, but I'd always dreamed of opening my own one day. I never wanted a big place, though; they all end up being too corporate. I got the opportunity to buy this place and I couldn't let it slip by me."

"You've done a fabulous job with it. I've noticed the before pictures on the walls."

"I wanted people to see what it what once and to have a reminder of all my hard work."

"You have lots of land with it. Do you plan to expand at any point?"

"Yes, I do actually. I'm in the process of arranging planning, so watch this space." She doesn't want to give too much away; I can understand that.

"I'd love to see what you do with the land. I will have to keep an eye on your website."

We both move on to talk to others. It was nice to get to talk to Holly some more. It was such a great afternoon/evening that I was glad to put my feet up at the end of it.

#

Chapter Ten

It's the day of the parade and there is a buzz everywhere that it is hard not to get caught up in it. It doesn't start until late this afternoon, so I spend the morning reading. I need the rest after my long walk yesterday and then the busy afternoon and evening. I've finished the book just in time to get ready to go. I will be needing a new book. This thought makes me smile, as I could be Hunter's first customer. I'm looking forward to seeing him at the parade. The feelings I have for him scare me a bit as we haven't known each other long. I know he likes me, but I'm not sure how much, whether it is just a fleeting romance or something more. I'm hoping it's something more to him than it is to me.

Everyone from the inn leaves together with lots of chatter. Hunter told me that he would meet me there after he was finished sorting out some more paperwork. The main road has been roped off and people are gathering along the paths. The town is busier today, with more visitors here for the parade, which adds to the atmosphere. This is the most people I have seen here but who doesn't love a good parade. I hear the parade before I can see it and Hunter joins me just in time. With the parade starting, there is no chance of talking; it is so loud. I watch the parade and will talk to Hunter later. He does put his arm around my waist though and I move closer to him.

There are drummers leading the parade, followed by people dressed as the twelve days of Christmas. It's a wonderful sight. Behind the twelve days is a truck carrying the winter formal queen from the local high school. She is in a silver ball gown and looks beautiful. The truck is decorated with white covers and silver flowers, with lots of twinkling lights.

Then, there's a truck carrying a life-sized gingerbread house made from wood, not that you can tell. It is decorated like a gingerbread house with white paint as icing, large fake sweets and lots of snow. After that is everyone from the nativity, including a pregnant Mary on a real donkey.

Last, there is a one-horse open sleigh with Santa sitting in the back waving at everyone. I would love to be able to take a ride in it. There is a lot of cheering that follows, along with everyone joining in the parade at the back to follow Santa to his grotto. Once there, the children line up to go and see him.

There are stalls around with beverages and food, all sending tantalising smells into the air. My tummy rumbles at the smell, but before I can say, shall we get something to eat, Hunter spins me around and kisses me, hard.

"Hi," Hunter says after catching his breath.

"Hi. I loved that, seeing everyone all dressed up and the drummers were fantastic."

"They are, aren't they. They've been leading the parade for years and just get better and better."

"I'm so glad I got to see it. I can't believe I've been here ten days all ready. It feels like it's going way too quickly."

"I'm glad you are enjoying yourself," Hunter says before kissing me again.

We then grab some food and go in search of a place to sit.

"Did you get all the paperwork sorted?" I'm curious to know how he got on.

"Mostly, just a couple more bits to sign and the shop will be all mine."

"I'm happy for you. Do you know when you are planning to open?"

"Not until the new year, as I want to repaint and sort out a seating area. I got a wonderful idea from someone the other day," Hunter says jokingly nudging me.

"Wonder who that was," I joke back, nudging him. "I'm happy to be of service. I think it will make a great addition to the place."

"It sure will."

Once we have finished eating, Hunter suggests we go to the bar. I'm happy to go. I've not actually been in there while I've been here. As we walk through the doors, we notice that a lot of people seemed to have the same idea as a crowd as already gathered.

We manage to find a spot where we can stand and chat. It is loud, but it's manageable to hear each other. All around us, people are discussing their favourite part of the parade and what shopping they still had to do. I'm glad not to be one of the last-minute shoppers this year. Hunter says he still has some shopping to do but not much, typical guy really.

I'm quite merry by the time Hunter walks me back to the inn. I had a great time and I had joined in with the singing and dancing, much to Hunter's amusement. Apparently, he doesn't dance, but he seemed to like watching me dance. The cold air helps to sober me up on the walk back and I lean into Hunter for support and the closeness walking back. We stand outside kissing for a while before we break apart and go in different directions. I could have easily asked him to come up, but I don't want our first time to be while I'm under the influence. Not that Hunter asked or anything; he is a gentleman.

#

Chapter Eleven

I wake up the next morning feeling a bit groggy, but it's nothing a hearty American breakfast can't cure. I don't know why I drank so much last night, but I am on holiday and it's not like I'm drinking all the time, is it. I really enjoyed singing and dancing with the fellow participants of the bar. It was a great night, and everyone was so friendly.

I've finished all the Christmas-themed activities that are available, so today I'm going to go to the ski slope. I'm not skiing, though; I'm not brave enough. They have sleds available, different types apparently and sledding always looks like fun. Hunter is going with me, which I'm looking forward to. He told me he used to be on the slopes a lot growing up. After breakfast and once I'm wrapped up all warm, I'm ready to go, and just in time has Hunter is wanting in the lobby for me.

"I didn't think the hill would be this high," I say while looking up at the top of it, which is hard to see.

"It's not too bad. You're not scared of sledding down, are you?" Hunter says, teasing me.

"No, no. OK, maybe a little. Stop laughing," I say while tapping him on the arm. "You're used to it; we have nothing like this in Wales."

"We can share sleds if you like?" I like this idea—any excuse to be near him.

It takes about twenty minutes to walk up the hill and pick out their sled and I'm slightly breathless by the time we make it up here.

"Wow, the view is amazing up here and it seems higher than when I looked at it from the bottom."

"I'll be holding you, so you won't fall off," Hunter says, squeezing me in a side hug.

"Let's do this." I put on a brave face and head to where everyone seems to start from.

Hunter gets me to sit in the front so he can sit behind me and hold on to me. He counts to three, then pushes off. At first, I keep my eyes closed, but I soon open them and enjoy the thrill of the ride down. It is exhilarating and once we reach the bottom, we roll off the sled and lie there smiling at each other.

"That was amazing. I can't believe I was a bit scared. What an absolute thrill. I can't wait to get back up to the top. This time, I want my own sled."

"I knew you'd like it. How about a race, then?" Hunter says, winking at me.

"You're on."

Hunter wins quite easily, so I insist on a rematch, but Hunter still wins. I need to win a least once, so we go up once more and I manage to just get to the bottom first. I'm thrilled I won and can't help but brag about it, even though Hunter has won more times than me. It was so much fun. I felt free while on the downfall. It's a great feeling.

"Thank you for bringing me. I have had so much fun," I say while I put my arms around Hunter.

"It was my pleasure. It was fun. I haven't done that in years," Hunter replies, smiling at me and then he kisses me.

We are on our way back to the inn and I decide to see how Hunter will react to the fact that I been thinking about moving here.

"So, I've been doing a bit of research into what moving out here will entail, not that I've made my mind up."

I watch him and his face lights up a bit even though I can tell he is trying to hide it. "Is there a lot to it?"

"More than you would think. Also, after a quick search, there are no jobs for me here, so I would have to move somewhere else."

At this, his face falls and we both know it's because he won't be able to move with buying the bookshop.

"It's a big decision to make and I know that we have something between us, but I can't just move for you. I need to do it for me too." I hope I haven't a fended him.

"I wouldn't expect you to, Emma. You need to do what is best for you. I agree that we do have something, and I would like to get to know you more, but I wouldn't like you to move for me and if it ended, then you would regret it or resent me for it." He seems to have put a lot of thought into it, which is good, as we seem to be on the same thinking level. We carry on walking in silence back to the inn. I think we are both lost in our own thoughts.

#

Once we get back to the inn, we sit on the porch swing drinking hot chocolate to warm ourselves up. We sit there for a while, and I end up leading my head on his shoulder. I'm so comfy under the blanket and leaning on his shoulder that I close my eyes for a while. I'm just stirring when I hear Holly's voice, so I decide to keep my eyes closed so she can talk to her nephew.

"Is she asleep?" Holly whispers.

"Yea, I think so. How are you, Aunt Holly?"

"I'm OK, getting ready for the party on Christmas Eve. How about you? You two seem to be spending quite a bit of time together."

"I'm OK. I'm happy, and Emma is a big part of that. We haven't known each other long, but I've never felt like this before. I don't want her to go home; I want us to have a chance. She told me before that she has started looking into coming over here, but she wants to do it for the right reasons and of all people I understand that."

"I've not seen you this happy before. I know you went through a bad time with Lana, and you can kind of emphasise with what Emma must be feeling. I just don't want you to get hurt when she goes home. Do you think she will stay?"

"I'm not sure. She said she has thought about it before this holiday, but it's a big move for her, and a lot of pressure on the relationship. What happens if she stays and we break up, I couldn't do that to her. She also said that she would need to be somewhere else for her job, which I can't blame her. She has worked hard to be an event manager and wouldn't want her to take just any job."

"I know it's hard, but she's not going yet, so you have time to figure it out. How's the shop coming along?"

"Last bit to do tomorrow. They close Christmas Eve, and then it's all mine."

"I'm proud of you, Hunter. Let me know if you need anything. I'm going to go in, in case she wakes up."

"Thanks, Aunt."

When I'm sure she has gone, I open my eyes and look at Hunter.

"Sorry, must have dozed off. I thought I heard you talking?"

"Holly was just here. It's OK. It'll be all that walking and sledding, tired you out," says Hunter while rubbing my arm. "How about we get some food and then get you back for an early night."

"Sounds like heaven. Thank you," I say and give Hunter a kiss.

I'm curious as to who Lana is and why he knows a bit of what I'm going through, but since I was pretending to still be asleep, I can't ask. I will just have to hope that in time, he will tell me. I'm glad he suggested an early night, as I could do with one.

\#

Chapter Twelve

It's Christmas Eve, and I wake up with a good feeling about today. Christmas Eve always puts me in a jolly mood and I'm looking forward to the party here tonight. The smell coming from downstairs is mouth-watering. Aromas of spices, turkey, ham and cookies, it certainly smells like a feast is being cooked and baked. I can't wait to see what delights there are.

I go for a morning walk to soak up the busy Christmas Eve atmosphere. People are shopping, chatting and there is still a Que to see Santa. It's not as busy as the shops get in Wales; there it always seems manic, and people are always pushing past you. Here, though, people are still pleasant and there is no rush about them. It makes for a much nicer experience.

My phone starts ringing and my stomach does a flip when I see Hunter's name flash across the screen.

"Hi." My smile is getting bigger.

"Hi. Can you meet me by the bookshop in half an hour?"

"Yea, sure. Everything OK?" I hope nothing is wrong.

"All good. I have a surprise for you."

"What is it?"

"It wouldn't be a surprise if I told you. I'll see you in thirty minutes."

"It was worth a try. See you soon."

The next thirty minutes, I spend in anticipation, so I keep myself occupied with going around the market. As I'm approaching the bookstore, I notice a one-horse, open sleigh on the ground across from the store. I wonder again what it would be like to be able to go for a ride in it. Then I spot Hunter talking to the driver, and he waves me over.

#

"Surprise!" says Hunter excitedly.

"This is my surprise?" I'm in shock.

"Yea. I thought you'd enjoy a ride. It's OK if you don't want to."

"Are you kidding, I 'd love to go for a ride in it." I throw my arms around Hunter and kiss him. I can't believe it. I'm going in a one-horse open sleigh! I feel like jumping up and down with joy, but I contain myself. I don't want to embarrass myself now, do I.

I'm pretty sure it's the sleigh from the parade. It's deep mahogany with bells and a lantern on either side. The horse is beautiful, chocolate brown, with a glossy coat. I take a picture of it and hop up in the cart. Hunter helps me get in, as it wasn't as easy as I thought. He then covers us both with the thick red blanket that is there. He puts his arm around me, and we set off heading towards the surrounding woods. It's an amazing experience, and it goes at a nice pace to be able to take in the surroundings. We travel around the out skirts of the town for an hour before heading back into town. People look at us as we pass them and some of them wave. I feel special to be able to experience this. I can't thank Hunter enough.

"This is amazing. Thank you."

"It's my pleasure. I thought it would be a great way to show you the surrounding areas. Plus, you can now say you've been on a one-horse open sleigh. How many people do you know who can say that?"

"None. It has been a dream of mine, but I never thought I'd be able to do it."

"I'm glad I was able to make one of your dreams come true," Hunter says, looking into my eyes. "I've arranged for us to be dropped off at the inn so you can get ready for tonight."

"Thank you. This has definitely been a big highlight of my holiday for me." I kiss him with as much passion as appropriate for being in public. He really is an amazing guy and I want more of him.

#

Once Hunter has left me at the inn, I'm in a hurry to get to my room to call Mum to tell her about the sleigh ride.

"It was amazing, Mum."

"It certainly sounds like it, love. You sound so happy and in love."

"I think I am, but what do I do about it?"

"What would you like to do about it? That's what you need to ask yourself."

"I want to see where it goes, but the distance, I would have to move out here. What do you think I should do?" I want my mum's advice and thoughts on me moving out here.

"I can't answer that for you, love, but what I will say is, follow your heart. I would miss you dearly, but I want you to be happy. You have talked about moving out there before, but make sure it's right for you." I can tell if she is trying not to cry, and it makes my throat go dry with emotion.

"Thanks, Mum, for understanding and for the advice and letting me decide for myself."

"That's what mums do. You could always move out there for a year to see how the relationship goes and whether you like it out there or not. I know you love it there now, but it will be different for the rest of the year."

"That does sound like a good idea. Me and Hunter haven't really talked about what's going to happen. We need to, though, but after the celebrations."

"Keep me up to date with what you are thinking."

"I will, Mum."

After talking some more, I promise to call her tomorrow to wish the family a happy Christmas. Then, I get ready for the party. I brought a red dress, especially for the occasion, with a black pair of kitten heels. I take time on doing my hair, adding waves, going for a different style. I feel a bit lighter after talking to my mum about potentially moving out here. I'm so happy that she will be on board, no matter what I decide, and her one-year idea is a good one.

#

Downstairs, the dining room has been moved around so that the tables are clubbed together with the food spread out on them. There are mini pizzas, Eggnog Cinnamon rolls, cranberry and Brie tartlets and sausage rolls. There is a Christmas tree made of cold meats and cheese; there are also mince pies and cookies for dessert. It all looks delicious, and I can't wait to tuck in.

In the living room area, some of the dining chairs have been added to give more seating. Christmas songs are playing on low in the background. Most of the guests are already here. Hunter is already there, too and he seems to spot me straight away. Like he can sense me, this thought sends a chill over my body in a good way.

"You look stunning."

"Thank you. You don't look so bad yourself," I say while looking him up and down. He has trousers and a shirt on, top two buttons undone, very handsome.

"Shall we go and mingle?" Hunter says, offering me his arm.

The atmosphere is great; everyone is friendly and in high spirits, more so than they have been all week. The food is as delicious as it looks, and I end up trying everything, which results in eating far too much. Hunter barley leaves my side as we spend the evening talking to each other and to the other guests.

After the remaining food has been taken away, there is dancing. Hunter happily dances with me to the slow music, and it feels nice to be in his arms. It makes me feel loved. It's a lovely evening and I feel just at home here in this place, and with Hunter.

At the end of the night, I get the present that I brought for Hunter and the card that I made. First, I give him the card.

"Thank you. It's lovely. You don't have to thank me for spending time with you. I have enjoyed every minute of it," Hunter says after reading the card.

"I have, too. I also got you a small gift. It's not much, but I hope you like it." I'm a bit nervous now about how he will react to it.

"You didn't have to, but thank you," He says, giving me a brief kiss before opening it eagerly. It's the bunting I got from the market.

"It's for your shop. You said you liked the name I suggested, and when I saw this, I thought it would look great in the shop. The lady who made it says she can make anything you like in that material, so you could have cushion covers. It feels a bit silly now." I start feeling embarrassed, with my face heating up to show it.

"I love it. It will go great on the counter. Thank you," Hunter says and kisses me again.

"I got you one more thing," I say, holding out another gift.

"It's amazing and looks just like the one we made," Hunter says, amazed at the snowman in his hands.

"The lady at the market said she makes some to order, so I thought of our snowman."

"I have got you something, but I'm planning on bringing it tomorrow when I come and see my aunt."

"You didn't have to get me anything, but thank you. Can't wait to see what it is."

I wasn't sure if I would be seeing him tomorrow, so I wanted him to have his presents tonight. I'm secretly glad that he thought to get me something, too. It goes to show what kind of man he is. We sit on the sofa, cuddled up with lots of kisses for a bit longer before Hunter really must get going. I am going to sleep soundly tonight, dreaming of a life with Hunter. I still can't believe I have met someone as wonderful has him. This is turning into the holiday dreams are made of.

#

Chapter Thirteen

Christmas morning arrives with more snowfall and an odd feeling in my stomach. It feels strange to wake up with no family and no presents to race downstairs to open. Still, I'm glad to be spending my Christmas here, but it is just a bit odd but something I would have to get used to if I moved. After getting ready into my Christmas-themed dress that I brought especially for today, I head downstairs. The plan is for everyone to meet at nine o'clock for breakfast. Once I'm at the table, my spirits are lifted with all the festive cheer. We all enjoy a hearty breakfast and then make for the living area.

"Thank you all for choosing to spend your Christmas with us. We are honoured. For those of you spending your first Christmas with us, this is the time we like to give out presents. Some of you have left presents under the tree and Santa has left presents for the children. There is a gift for everyone, so let's begin," Holly says. She then sets about handing out the presents, starting with the children first.

It's a special experience to witness the joy of others opening their gifts. I'm overwhelmed when Holly gives me a present. I eagerly unwrap it to find a brown scrapbook. On the front is a picture of the inn with the words 'My Mistletoe Christmas'. I open it to find candid photos of me at the inn. There are ones of the activities that I joined in. I was aware of Holly taking them at the time, but I didn't think anything of it. There are also ones of the town, the market and the parade.

Also, inside are some photos of me and Hunter; he must have given them to his aunt. This is a gift that I will cherish forever. By the time I had looked through it all, my eyes were filled with tears.

After that, we have a few hours to ourselves before lunch would be ready. I use this time to go to my room to give my family a call. I'm more emotional today talking to my mum, and so is she. It's our first Christmas apart. I tell her all about the scrapbook that Holly has made for me and that the other new guests got one, too. Mine was extra special, as it has pictures of me and Hunter together. I got to hear all about the gifts everyone back home has had and how everyone is doing. After the call ends, I lay on my bed for a while, getting my emotions under control. I must have fallen asleep because I'm startled when there is a knock on the door.

I rush to the door, thinking I must be late for lunch, and I'm taken aback when Hunter is on the other side.

"Merry Christmas, Emma."

"Merry Christmas, Hunter. I thought it was Holly coming to tell me I'm late for lunch."

"Just me, and you're not late for lunch."

"I came up to ring my family, which was emotional. I must have fallen asleep," I say as I check my hair to make sure it's not sticking up anywhere.

"You look lovely."

"The scrapbook your Auntie gave me is wonderful. Have you seen it?"

"No, I haven't. I know she does them though, as she likes to make sure that all the guests have a gift to open on Christmas morning."

I invite him in and show him the book. We sit on the bed, looking at it.

"I wondered why she wanted the photos. She said it was for a project. I should have known. I have your gift."

I take the present and carefully unwrap it. Inside is a long black velvet box, which I carefully open to revel a silver chain with a delicate snowflake on it. I'm overwhelmed with it; I wasn't expecting anything like this. It gives me more hope that his feelings for me are strong, too.

"It's absolutely gorgeous. Thank you."

"It's just like you, then," Hunter says, looking into my eyes. "As soon as I saw it, I knew I had to get it for you. I loved the look in your eyes when you saw the first snowfall and then again every time, I see you."

"I don't know what to say except thank you." I kiss Hunter and look into his eyes. "I'm falling in love with you," I blurt out and instantly go red in the face. I don't know what made me confess that at this moment, but it felt right. I'm about to say that I shouldn't have said that when Hunter kisses me and it is a kiss filled with so much promise.

"I'm falling in love with you, too." Then he kisses me again and that one leads to another. It's a like a fire has gone off between us and we need each other to survive. All sense of time goes as we take our time to explore each other. The passion is out of this world. I have never connected so closely with someone before; it felt like our bodies were made for each other. I'm diffidently in trouble now, as I don't think I can let him go.

#

We emerge from my room nearly an hour later to go and join the others, having a drink before lunch begins. Hunter goes off in search of his aunt, as he didn't really talk to her when he got here. He just came to find me. I go and get myself a drink and reflect on the past hour, which has been amazing. We connected perfectly, our bodies in sync. Thinking about it, I can feel myself getting hot, so I finish my drink to cool me down. Hunter joins me as I get another drink and snakes his arm around my waist, which sends tingles through my body. Holly comes in then and calls everyone into the dining room for lunch.

The table looks spectacular with a Christmas-themed cloth and candles intertwined with holly down the middle. The aromas in here smell heavenly and my stomach grumbles agreeing with me. There are plates in everyone's setting and they are lovely with an image of holly all around the edge with a red trim to them. Holly brings out plates with a turkey and then sets about handing out bowls of vegetables for everyone to help themselves. All of the serving dishes are in the same pattern too, which brings it all together, in my opinion.

It's a lovely family atmosphere, with us handing around all the trimmings. As well as vegetables, there are pigs in blankets and roast potatoes, with gravy and cranberry sauce. The mash potato is heavenly, creamy and the best I've tasted. The whole spread is spectacular and all around the table there is chatter and laughter. I don't feel like I'm missing out on anything back home as this like one big family and we are all getting along. I have Hunter at my side, and we keep sharing little glances at each other. When we only need to use one hand, the other hands find each other, so we spend a lot of the time holding hands under the table. I can't believe how happy

I am, and full, I think I've overdone it on the gorgeous food. Then again, that's nothing new. I always overeat on the main meal. I think everyone does. It's like some unwritten rule.

Hunter helps his aunt to clear away the dishes. I did offer to help, but he insisted that I go and relax. It was nice that Holly joined us for the meal. It was nice to be able to get to know her a bit more. I find myself a comfy seat and watch everyone around me. The children are playing with their new toys, and some have even gone out for a walk.

#

The afternoon is full of games and more laughter. We all play charades, which turns into one big laugh fest. That is followed by a couple of board games. People filter in and out when the board games are being played; it's a nice, relaxed atmosphere with games going on if you want to join in. No one is expected to join in or be made to feel guilty if they choose not to. It's just nice to be surrounded by people and join in when we want to. This is what Christmas is meant to be: fun and laughter with friends and family and if you can't be with them then with the people who are around you.

Early evening, we settle in to watch a movie in the lounge area and nibble on the leftovers from lunch. Hunter and I are cuddled up on the love chair, enjoying the film and being together. I might have started the day with a sad feeling of being away from my family, but I am definitely ending it on a high. It has been a special day with great company and a wonderful experience.

#

Chapter Fourteen

Boxing day starts with a well-earned lie-in. I'm in no hurry to get breakfast, as I eat far too much yesterday. There isn't much planned today, mainly relaxation. After a very light breakfast, I go for a walk into town to burn off some of the extra calories from yesterday and to see what it is like on boxing day in the town. Back in Wales, the shops will be mayhem with people trying to get their hands on a bargain in the sales. It's completely different here, with only the essential shops open. It's nice that they all get an extra day off for the holidays; this is how it should be, being able to recover from the big day and see more family and friends.

Hunter is seeing his parents in Maine today. From the day after tomorrow, he is going to start sorting out the bookshop, as he needs to open as soon as he can, which is understandable. He can't spend all his time with me. He wants to paint it and make room for a sofa and a couple of chairs. I could always help him paint. I don't have much planned for this week. Actually, that sounds like a good idea, and we can get to know each other more.

At the inn, I join the family who are watching a Christmas film, while enjoying a hot chocolate and mince pie. Once the film finishes, I go up to my room to call my mum.

"Hi, love. How was yesterday for you? It was strange not having you here."

"Hi, Mum. It was strange, but I had a great day in the end. The food was amazing; we played games and watched a film."

"Did you see Hunter?"

"I did. He got me a beautiful snowflake necklace. He also told me that he is falling in love with me. I told him I was, too."

"I'm happy for you, love. I'm sad for me. Does this mean you want to move out there?" Mum asks and I can tell she trying to keep her emotions out of her voice.

"I'm not sure, Mum. It would be simple if we were in the same country. I really don't know what to do. He hasn't asked me to stay, though. Does that mean he doesn't?" I hadn't thought of that until just now. I'm sure he wants me to move.

"I would think he would like you to stay, but he knows this is your decision and a hard one. He probably doesn't want to put pressure on you. You need to talk to him about it. You are only there for one more week."

"You're right, Mum. You always know what to say." I instantly feel better.

"That's what mums do. Now go and enjoy yourself; we'll speak soon."

#

Back downstairs, Holly has put out a buffet of more of the leftovers from yesterday as well as some fresh things. It feels just like it is at home; this is what I normally do on boxing day. I talk to some of the guests to see what they have planned for the week. It turns out that those who aren't going home in a couple of days are going skiing. I still don't feel confident enough to give it a try. Sledging was fun, but I think I will

82

leave it as that for the time being. Maybe some time in the future, I could learn to ski. I didn't plan anything for this week, just relaxing and site seeing, as I did so much before Christmas.

Wanting some fresh air, I go for a walk into town and I end up sitting by the big tree. Watching the world go by, I contemplate what live would be like if I moved out here. The romance of it is very tempting, but I've got to think practically. I will need a place to live, somewhere to work. These won't be easy to find in a town like this. I haven't seen any to let signs or job postings around town or further afield for my type of work. Without these things, I don't know how I can move out here, even for a year to test the waters. For that, I would at least need some sort of job to start me off with while I look for an event management one. Was this move just for Hunter? I didn't want to accept that; I do love it here and I have dreamed of moving out here before. I would spend as much time as possible with Hunter this week, in case it was the end for us. I also need to make sure I make the right move for me, which requires more thought.

With that thought, I get up and walk around for a bit before going back to the inn. When I get there, the two families that are staying there are outside making snowmen. The kids shout to me to join in, there such sweet kids, so I decide to join in. My mood is soon lifted, and we end up having a snowball fight with two teams. My team wins. We get to pick the film to watch. I let Bella choose, but she insists on my help, so who am I to say no.

"What's your favourite film?" Bella asks me as we go through the films.

"Miracle on 34th Street. What's yours?"

"The Santa Clause. I like the first one, then the third and the second one last. It's still good, but I prefer the others."

"Is that what we are going to watch?"

"Yes. Which one is your favourite out of the three?"

"The first one."

"We will watch that one, then."

When we are ready, Holly has the hot chocolates waiting to warm us up and of course they are topped with cream on marshmallows, much to the kids delight. I have a lovely afternoon and it has taken my mind of things, for a while at least.

I'm just thinking about getting some food when Hunter walks in carrying pizza for everyone, his aunt's orders apparently. I'm so happy to see him that my cheeks ache from smiling so much by the time he has sorted the pizza out and come over to kiss me. We spend the evening talking to the others and at some point, one of the children asked for the karaoke machine to be on, but it is now way past when they went to bed and me, Hunter, Holly and a couple of others are still singing away. I have no idea how many gins I've had, but I do know that I have had a great time. I'm not the best singer, but it doesn't matter. It's the fun that counts. That's what I tell myself anyway.

Chapter Fifteen

The next morning, I wake up to find Hunter is already washed and dressed and has a cheeky grin on his face.

"Morning, gorgeous," Hunter says, bending down to kiss me good morning.

"Morning. I could get used to waking up to this."

"I have a surprise for you. All you need is your passport."

"Where are we going? Wait. I don't have any spare money to travel anywhere by plane."

"No need to worry. It's my treat, and it's a surprise."

I get ready as quickly as I can with Hunter offering advice on what kind of shoes I should put on. With breakfast ready for me to take with me, Hunter eats his before I got up apparently, we head out in Hunter's car. All I have managed to get out of Hunter is that it won't take long to get there. Hunter has even managed to get us checked in without me finding out where we are going. The one thing he can't control, though, is the overhead speaker announcing that our flight is ready to board.

"This is us," Hunter says, taking hold of my hand.

"New York? OMG. Really?" I'm in shock.

"Yep. You said it's somewhere else you would like to see at Christmas, so here we are."

"I don't know what to say. Thank you doesn't seem to be enough."

"The look on your face is thanks enough. Plus, I can think of one or two ways you can thank me later," Hunter says winking at me. "It will be a long day with flying back this evening, but I wanted to take you."

"I don't mind."

We board the flight. It's a small plane, but I'm too delirious to take much in. We fly to LaGuardia Airport and from there we grab a taxi to the Empire State Building where we are starting our day. Hunter has the whole day planned, with us only being here for a short time.

#

I don't let go of Hunter's hand. The sheer number of people on the streets is overwhelming. I knew it would be busy, but not as manic as this and people don't seem to mind who they walk into. I'm glad I didn't come here instead, as I don't think I could cope with these streets for more than a couple of days. You can smell the fumes from the sheer number of cars on the road, more than there is in London, at least on the day I was there. It's not all bad, though, as the decorations are everywhere as you'd expect, and they look fantastic.

The Empire State Building is way bigger than I anticipated. I mean obviously I knew it would be huge, but still, looking at it in person is on a different scale. Built in the 1920s, it is an impressive art deco skyscraper with shops and restaurants on its bottom floors. My neck is hurting, as I'm taking it all in.

"Shall we go in?" Hunter asks while he squeezes my hand.

"Yes, please," I manage to say, as I'm momentarily speechless.

Once we enter and join the Que for tickets, I take in the marble foyer. It has Christmas lights hanging from the ceiling with silver stars in between. I'm in awe as we wait. When we get to the front, we get tickets to go to the Main Observatory, which is on the 86th floor. You can go to the Top Deck on the 102nd floor. This costs a bit more and seems a bit too high for me. Just going to the Main Observatory will be more than OK for me.

Stepping out of the elevator, my breath is taken away by the view. The breeze might have something to do with it too. We are lucky we have a clear day, as we can see for miles. I can even see the Statue of Liberty. I've forgotten all about the breeze and the temperature drop, as I'm totally amazed by this view. I must have taken hundreds of photos.

"Thank you for bringing me here, Hunter," I say as I put my arms around his neck and kiss him.

"It's my pleasure, Emma. I've actually only been up here once. This view really is something."

We stand arm in arm, taking it all in before it's time to head back down. We then walk along Broadway to Times Square and the Theatre District.

There are lots of big screens everywhere advertising anything and everything, making it a vibrant place. We walk around for a while, as I take in the different billboards and names of shows. The Christmas decorations are different here, which enhance the surroundings. I can see the appeal of the place, but it's too busy and noisy for me. My stomach starts to grumble, so we head off to a street vendor that Hunter says sells the best hot dogs in the area. We then carry on our way, with our next stop being Rockefeller Centre and the iconic Christmas tree.

It's bigger than anything I could have imagined. It's so busy you can't get close to it, but I don't mind because at least I can see it and that is enough.

"It is wonderful and so much bigger than it looks on TV." I'm mesmerised by it; it's so colourful.

"I'm glad you've been able to see it," Hunter says, putting his arm around my waist.

Once I have finished taking in the impressive tree, Hunter takes me to the Chanel Gardens. These are beautiful and have a row of glowing angels, which I imagine look spectacular when lit up. The smells coming from all the plants and flowers have a calming aroma to them. The ice rink is as big as you'd expect and full of people having fun. There is a wonderful atmosphere around here, with people skating and admiring the tree. There are loads of international flags lining the building, which is home to Saturday Night Live and the Today Show. You could spend hours here taking in all the sites and shops.

It's mid-afternoon when we get to central park where we can go ice skating at the Wollman rink. It is so much bigger than the one in Mistletoe and with no decorations in the middle. We skate for an hour before taking a walk around the park. It's amazing that this place is here in the middle of New York, and you can't tell where you are, either. I could spend a whole day just walking around the park. It's peaceful, but then busy in some areas.

We have a look around the Strawberry Fields, a beautiful garden built in memory of John Lennon. We also come across the Hans Christian Anderson statue. This is lovely with him sitting down with a book looking at the ducking that is on the floor; it's like he is reading the story to it. It's a heart-warming memorial to the man of many great children's books.

I also get to see Belvedere Castle from a distance and Hunter points out where the zoo roughly is. You really do need a couple of days just to explore central park. It's a spectacular place, and it still amazes me that it is in the middle of a bustling city. New York is really a diverse place. I'm glad I have had the chance to see just a small part of it.

"Thank you so much for bringing me here," I say while putting my head on Hunter's shoulder as we sit on a park bench.

"It's my pleasure. I'm just sorry it's so rushed. Maybe we could come again next year, maybe."

"That would be lovely. I can see why you prefer Christmas in Mistletoe. I mean, it is lovely here, but it's too busy for me. I'm glad I didn't pick here to stay for three weeks, as I don't think I would have enjoyed it the same."

"Or you wouldn't have met me."

"That, too. Days out or a weekend here would be lovely, so we're not rushing the same. I really do appreciate you showing me around here."

I am falling more and more in love with him. Now all I have to do is to come up with a plan and, more importantly, talk to Hunter about it, but not today I want to enjoy our little getaway. After walking to a pretzel vendor, we get a taxi back to the airport. I've had a lovely day, but it has been long and I'm glad to be going back.

Back in Burlington, Hunter drives us back to Mistletoe and I end up falling asleep in the car.

"Emma, wake up. We're back."

I slowly open my eyes and dreamily look at Hunter. Then I realise that we are still in his car.

"Sorry for falling asleep."

"It's no problem. Do you want me to carry you in?"

"As nice as that sounds, I will be OK to walk." It was tempting, but it would be embarrassing if anyone saw us. We kiss goodbye, and I go straight to sleep as soon as my head hits the pillow.

The next morning, I'm feeling overwhelmed by the last twenty-four hours, so I call my mum to talk to her.

"Hi Mum, sorry I didn't call yesterday. Hunter took me away for a surprise day out."

"It's OK, darling. That sounds lovely. Where did he take you?"

"New York!"

"Wow, that was generous of him."

"It was. He planned the whole day; it was amazing. We saw the tree, went ice skating, central park and looked at some shops."

"Sounds like you had a fabulous time."

"I did. I can't believe he did that for me. I love him, Mum." It sinks in, then I do love him, and I want to find a way to stay or at least come back soon.

"It sounds like he feels the same way."

"Are you OK, Mum?" There is a crack in her voice.

"Yes, love. I'm so happy for you and sad at the same time because I think you've decided what to do, haven't you?"

"I'm sorry, Mum. He makes me so happy. I still need to talk to him about it, though." I hope my decision doesn't hurt my mum too much. I know it will be hard, for both of us.

"No need to apologise, love. I want you to be happy, and if that means moving to America, then I fully support that," Mum says encouragingly.

"Thanks, Mum. You'd be able to come out and visit and we will visit you. Plus, it would take a few months to get my visa," I say, feeling a little sad at that.

I can't wait to call this my home. We say our goodbyes, and I can't wait any longer to go and see Hunter. First, though, I need to find some clothes that I don't mind painting in so that I can help him when I get there.

#

On my way there, I call in at the café to get some pastries and drinks to take over with me. I'm just about to knock on the door when it opens.

"Now, it's my turn," Hunter says after nearly bumping into me.

"Only fair. I've brought refreshments and a little something else."

"You must have read my mind. That's where I was just heading to."

"Great minds," I say, pointing from my head to his. "I've also changed into something I don't mind painting in."

"You don't have to, but thank you." He sounds grateful for the help.

Drinks and pastry finished, we crack on with the painting. Hunter has picked a warm cream colour to brighten the place up. At the moment, the walls are brown, so it may take two coats to cover. We talk about New York, and I thank him again.

"How would you feel if I look into getting a visa and moving out here?" I blurt out while I have the nerve to ask.

"I would be delighted," Hunter says, putting his brush down.

"Yea?"

"Yes," Hunter replies reassuringly. We carry on painting for moment before Hunter says, "I hope you don't mind, but I've actually had a friend look into for me. He does this for a living."

"I don't mind. That's helpful actually because it looks like a lot of paperwork, and I wouldn't know where to start." I'm thankful for the help.

"The basics of what he told me are that you need a job and somewhere to live for the application."

"I thought as much. How am I meant to find a job and a home? It's like it's going to be over between us before we have a real chance." I'm feeling exasperated.

"I thought that, but then I realised that I have the solution to both problems," he says with a grin on his face.

"I don't think it will be a good idea for me to move in with you. I love you, but we will want our own space to see how the relationship goes," I say, trying not to hurt his feelings.

"I love you too, but you're right. That's not what I thought, though. I have a flat above the shop. I hadn't even thought about it, then I realised it would be perfect for you. That is, if you like it and want it."

"Really? That would be amazing. That just leaves finding a job." This just might work.

"I can help with that, too. I need someone to run this place with me. Before you say it would be too much trying our relationship and working together, we don't necessarily have to work together. We could do shifts, work together sometimes; we can work it out."

"You've put a lot of thought into this."

"Maybe a little," Hunter says with a smile. "What do you think?"

"It sounds great. One thought I had was trying to find work for a year to give us time and time for me to get a real feel for the place, as it's such a big move," I say, putting my other idea out there.

"That sounds sensible, but I think you will love it here and we will work great together. You did name the place and come up with the seating idea, after all," he says, winking at me.

"I did, didn't I. I'm glad we have talked about this and that we are on the same page." I feel like a weight has been lifted.

"Me too. Is that a yes then to you coming and working here?" Hunter says with hope in his voice.

"My heart says yes, but I need a bit more time to make sure. It's not a no though; I just want to make the right decision as it is a lot for me to do, to uproot and move out here. I hope you understand."

"Of course, I do, Emma. You take all the time you need— just hopefully not too much time," Hunter says and gives me hug.

Conversation moves on and Hunter tells me of some new authors he plans to stock and that he is thinking of looking into doing author events.

"That sounds great, and it will definitely bring in more customers."

"It will, and there are different ways to go about it. It will also attract more visitors in the spring and summer months."

"It should do. Are those months generally quitter?" I ask curiously.

"They can be compared to the winter."

"I'll come and help you paint tomorrow, too, if you like."

"That would be great, but only if you don't mind."

"I don't mind at all, but I was thinking of going into Burlington the day after tomorrow to get a feel for the place. Unless you need me to help you some more?"

"No, no, that's OK. You go and explore. It'll be good for you. You've helped me today day, which I really appreciate, and you said you will again tomorrow. I want you to go and explore, especially with you thinking of moving out here. You need to know what's around you."

"Are you sure you'll be OK on your own, I don't mind."

"I'm sure," Hunter says while giving me a kiss. "How about you come back to mine after we finish up for the day and I'll cook for you."

"That sounds wonderful. Thank you."

#

I'm glad we had that tough conversation and as much as I wanted to say yes, I still need to talk it over more with my mum and come to the right decision for me. I did think that things might have gotten awkward between us after the discussion, but it didn't. We still had fun and talked loads.

It's nice being at his place. I get to see a different side to him, more relaxed. He has a large selection of books and films. It's a nice house that has been modernised inside with the latest gadgets but still keeping its charm. I could see us living here and raising a family. Far too early to be thinking this, but it just popped in my mind as I was walking around his place.

"Do you mind if I get a quick shower first, then I'll cook us a stir fry," Hunter says as he watches me looking at his book selection.

"No problem."

"You can always join me. I have some joggers and a sweater you can put on, if you like."

I don't need asking twice; I grab his hand and follow him to the bathroom. It's anything but a quick shower as we take our time washing each other, which then leads to shower sex. It's the best shower I've had. We help each other dry, and Hunter finds me some clothes to put on.

I help him make the stir fry by chopping the vegetables while he starts the chicken off. It feels natural to be working together in the kitchen and we move in harmony. We sit down on the sofa, a flick through the channels. The stir fry is delicious; Hunter is a great cook. We choose a film to watch and cuddle up. We are halfway through the film when the front doorbell rings. I pause the film while Hunter answers the door. The next minute, a blonde lady comes bursting into the living room.

"Who are you?" asks the women rather abruptly. "Never mind, Hunter, who's this?" she asks again without giving me a chance to answer.

"I'm Emma," I say before Hunter answers.

"Doesn't this look very cosy," says the lady after looking around the room.

With both of us looking at him expectantly, he finds his voice. "Emma, this is Lana. Lana, Emma."

"But who is she and why is she having a cosy night in with my fiancé?" asks Lana.

"Fiancé?" I whisper, shocked.

"Ex-fiancé. Lana, I told you it was over when I moved."

"No, you said you couldn't do the long-distance thing, so you moved here while I found a job, and here I am," Lana says matter of factually.

"I'm going to go. You two obviously have a lot to talk about," I say while picking up my stuff and rush out the door.

"Emma! It's not what it looks like; we broke up," Hunter says, catching up with me.

"I can't do this right now. You need to go back in there to her!" With that, I walk as quickly as I can back to the inn.

I'm in tears by the time I get there, and I go straight to my room, avoiding the looks by the guests. I lay on my bed for a while, unable to believe what happened tonight. I thought he loved me. I was about to move my whole life for him. How many lies has he been telling me? I end up crying myself to sleep.

#

Chapter Sixteen

I'm in a daze the following morning and not sure what to do with myself, as I was planning on painting with Hunter again. That's well and truly out the window. I know I properly need to speak to him at some point before I go. I can't see myself staying now, not without a proper job. I can't possibly work for Hunter and live in his flat after last night. I still can't believe that he is or was engaged. Surely, that is something he should have shared with me, especially knowing that I was thinking of moving here. A big part of me wants to believe him when he said she was his ex-fiancée but with her turning up with bags and all, what am I meant to think.

I'm fed up with mopping around at the inn, as I'm sure the guests are too, so I decide to go to the café for a change of scenery. The last person I wanted to see there was Lana. She's standing in the que, a couple of people ahead of me. Now that I look at her, she is gorgeous, with long blonde hair, stylishly dressed with an air of importance about her. I look nothing like her. If she is Hunter's type, what was he doing with me. She is at the counter now and I can hear her talking familiarly to the girl serving.

"I stayed at Hunter's last night, so I thought I'd get us some breakfast," Lana is saying.

"Are you two back together then?" says the cashier.

"We never really broke up; it was a misunderstanding. I'm going to be working in Burlington in the New Year." Lana informs her. "Can you believe that he had a woman at his place for tea last night. He said it was a thank you for helping him paint his new shop, but I think she thought it was more or wanted it to be. Like she would have a chance with him."

I want to turn around and walk out; I've heard enough, but I don't want to cause a scene or give Lana the satisfaction. She doesn't know that I'm standing here; at least I don't think she does. Just then, Lana turns around and sees me.

"No hard feelings about last night. I don't know what Hunter was thinking, probably trying to punish me. Anyway, I'm here now, so we can get back on track," says Lana in a jolly voice and walks out.

I don't know what to say, so I just nod and wait to be served. With my coffee and pastry in hand, I go and sit in the gazebo by the tree. I'm not in the mood for company or to have everyone in the cafe looking at me. How had I been so stupid. It had felt real and there were no signs that there was someone else. We hadn't talked about past partners, really, but I would have thought he would say if he was once engaged. I can't get my head around it.

I sit for a while breathing in the fresh air and the smell of the tree, which still smells wonderful. I look out towards the shops where I know the bookstore is, wondering if Lana is helping Hunter paint today and having fun like we did. Then I notice a figure running towards me. It has to be Hunter, so I get up intending to go back to the inn.

"Emma. Please stay and talk to me. It's not what it looks like," he says with a pleading look in his eyes.

"Really? That's not what Lana is telling everyone. She says you never broke up and it was a misunderstanding and that she is staying with you."

"What? That's not true, Emma. We are broken up; she just won't expect it. I thought she had, but now that she has heard that I brought a bookshop, she says she wants me back. I don't want her though. I never really did; it just took me a while to realise that. Since meeting you, I also knew that I didn't really love her cos what I feel for you is more than anything I felt for her. Please believe me."

"So, none of what she is saying is true? You didn't just cook for me as a thank you. She didn't stay at your place and is still staying there."

"Of course, I didn't cook for you as just a thank you. You know that."

"You're avoiding the question of where she is stopping." I need to know that that part isn't true, either.

"Yes, she stayed last night and will be tonight. She has nowhere to go."

"There's the inn," I say sarcastically.

"She turned up too late for a room last night and I didn't think it would be a good idea for her to be in the inn with you."

"You're right about that, but there is another the other side of the town."

"I can't just kick her out. We have too much history for that, but I swear there is nothing going on between us. I told you I loved you and I meant it. Please believe me."

"I don't know what to believe." With that, I walk off, leaving him standing there. This is a lot to deal with, but if they are truly over, then why is she staying with him. They might have history, but if they are broken up then that was for a reason so surely, he wouldn't want her in his house. I feel like screaming, but I manage to hold it in; instead, I kick snow about.

When I get back to the inn, Holly is waiting to see me.

"Emma, just the person. Do you have time for a chat?" Holly asks as I walk in.

"Yea, sure." I wipe my eyes to make sure you can't tell that I have been crying.

"Let's go to my office so we can talk with no interruptions." This has intrigued me. I thought it would be about Hunter.

"Is everything OK?" I ask once we are inside Holly's office.

"Yes, nothing to worry about, relax," Holly says, noticing that I have tensed up. "I have a proposition for you," Holly says in a light tone.

"OK. I'm listening." I'm intrigued as to what this could possibly be, and I take a seat.

"Right, well, I'll get right to it so not to take up too much of your time. You've seen the few events I put on over Christmas and I'm looking at expanding them. Not just at Christmas, but all year round. I've also looked into holding weddings here, as we have the land to expand on. I've been able to secure funding for a barn and a couple of self-contained huts. What I'm looking for is someone to run the events side of things. I'm OK on a small scale, but I need someone who knows what they are doing and can help me expand my business. What do you think so far?"

"I think it sounds wonderful. There is so much potential that can be done with a purpose-built barn and the whole place is wonderful. I think you'll be able to make it well worth your while," I say, and I can tell my face as lit up with all the prospects of the place.

"I was hoping that you'd think that. Hunter tells me that you are an events planner and manager, and that the company you worked for has merged, making you redundant. I've done my research and phoned your old boss, and she couldn't talk more highly of you. Hunter also told me that you are thinking of moving out here. I know he has offered you a job at his bookstore, but you are worth a whole more than that. I'm hoping that you will consider working for me?"

"Thank you for the very kind offer, but that move won't be happening now," I say as tears fill my eyes.

"What's happen? What has my nephew done? I'm sure you can work it out," Holly says.

"I don't know how with him already being engaged," I say and the tears start to fall.

"Are you talking about Lana? That's over," Holly says, sounding sincere.

"Not now; she has moved here. She turned up at his place last night."

"I am so sorry, Emma, but I'm sure there must be a good explanation. It is definitely over between them. I won't go into details, as it's not my place, but know that it is over. I've seen the way he looks at you; he loves you and way more than he did Lana."

"Sorry, he's your nephew, so maybe this isn't a good idea," I say, getting up out of her chair.

"Don't go. No more talk about Hunter. Promise. The job offer is still there, though. You're just what I'm looking for and I can tell you love the place. Were you just moving for him or is it for you too? This should be a move that is for you.

You would be in charge of all the events and there's a permanent room here for you, so you'd have somewhere to live, and rent free. I'd also be able to help with the visa and get it through quicker."

"It wasn't just for him. It has been a dream of mine to move out here. Plus, this town feels like home, but that could just be because of how much I love Christmas. The offer of free board is very appealing as well as the job itself; it's a dream job. I would need to speak to my mum and really think about it. When do you need answer by?"

"Before you leave would be great. I won't advertise the job till you go or say no. Think about it, talk to your mum. This is a big decision for you and make sure it's one that you want for you."

"I will do. Thank you so much." I get up to go.

"Emma, don't give up on Hunter, either," Holly says and gives me a weak smile.

#

I can't believe that just happened. A job offer and a place to live. I'm in shock. I can't believe Hunter told her about my work experience, in a good way, though. It's reassuring that she has rang my old boss to verify me and has not offered me this because of Hunter. If this offer had been at home in Wales, I wouldn't be thinking about it; I would just accept. That's where the problem lies; it seemed like an easier choice when Hunter was in the equation. I remember what Holly had asked. Was I moving for Hunter or myself. It has always been a pipe dream of mine to live in the States, but I never thought it would happen. Hunter had made it real, but now it's real without Hunter or any man. I don't need his job offer or his flat; I could do this all on my own. I need to think about it, as it is a real job offer that I don't have back home. I call my mum to tell her and get her advice.

"Hi, Mum."

"Hi, love, how are you?" Mum sounds happy to hear my voice.

"I'm OK, Mum. I want to talk to you about something."

"That sounds ambiguous."

"I've been offered a job running the events of a new purpose-built unit on the grounds of the inn. It will be to organise and run all the events to help the owner expand. Plus, she has offered me a room here for free."

"That sounds wonderful, love."

"Holly is expanding and needs an event coordinator."

"OK. What are you thinking? You will have a job, then if you are staying to be with Hunter."

"About that, Hunter's ex-girlfriend showed up and let's just say we aren't really talking at the moment," I say, trying to brush over the topic of Hunter.

"I'm sorry, love. Is he getting back with her?" Mum says with concern.

"No, he says it's over and has been for ages, but she didn't get the message apparently."

"So, you don't need to find a job there, then, if you're not staying?" Mum says in a hopeful tone.

"That's the thing. After talking to Holly and doing a lot of thinking, I'm not sure what to do. I need to move for me and not a guy, but I need to work out if I really want to make that move."

"And do you?"

"It's a once-in-a-lifetime opportunity, and I do love it here."

"Do you think you can make the move out there and make it work?"

"I do. It's a job I'd love to have. I've had a look online, and there aren't many jobs going by us."

"You can't just take a job halfway around the world because it's convenient. You need to be committed, not just for you but for your employer too."

"I understand all that, and a big part of me wants to take the job, but it's a long way from you and everyone else."

"I will stand by you, whatever you decide, and we would talk all the time. You will get holidays and I will too. When do you need to give Holly your answer?"

"Before I leave, she won't advertise for the job unless I turn it down."

"Has she only offered because she thought you were going to stay for Hunter?" Mum asks out of concern.

"No, Mum. Hunter told her what I do, and she looked up my old company and even rang my boss to see if I would be suitable for the job. She says the offer is there either way." I tell Mum reassuringly.

"That's good then, and good that she has looked into you and thinks you are cable of the position. It would be a big change for you, but I know you could do the job."

"Apparently, Amy sang my praises, which is good of her."

"So, she should. You are excellent at your job."

"Thanks, Mum."

"If you were offered the job and it was at home, would you think about taking it or just accept it there and then?"

"I'd accept." I didn't even need to think; I knew the answer.

"You said that with certainty. I think you know your answer, don't you?"

"Are you sure you're OK with it?"

"Yes, you do what is best for you. Take another day to be sure; you don't fly out till the 2nd. Really think about it, without Hunter in the equation, even if he does end up back in it."

"OK, I will do, Mum. I'm going into Burlington tomorrow; that way I will get a feel for the nearest big town. I know I love it in this town put. I will need other places to go to and not feel like I'm stuck here."

"I know you will do what is best for you and that you will give it a lot of thought. You've always had a good head on your shoulders. Have fun tomorrow and I'll speak to you soon."

"Thanks, Mum. Love you."

I take myself out for a walk to help clear my head and get some perspective. I'm having a rest on a bench by the big tree. Luckily, Hunter hasn't come across to me this time, when I get an urge to write down all the ideas that have popped into my head while I've been out. I haven't been able to stop thinking of ideas for events that we could put on and the different themes. I need to get it all wrote down, so I head to the shop to get a notepad and then go back to the inn and sit in the dining room.

Once there, I write down all the ideas that came to me; these include activities that can be held in the new barn. Ideas keep coming while I'm writing that I don't realise the time until Holly brings me a bowl of soup and bread roll.

"Thought you might be hungry, you look lost in thought. I didn't want to disturb you," Holly says, putting the bowl and plate down.

"Thank you. I hadn't noticed the time."

"Can I ask what you're writing?" Holly asks curiously.

"Of course. It's a list of the activities that I thought could be held in the new barn. Also, things that you would need to include in the barn and supplies that you will need," I say enthusiastically.

"You have been busy. Does this mean you are thinking of taking my offer?" Holly asks hopefully.

"Thinking, but only thinking, at the moment. It is a wonderful opportunity." I don't want to get Holly's hopes up too much.

"I'm glad you are thinking about it. This needs to be a decision you make for yourself. Have you spoken to your mum about it?"

"Yes, I have. She says she will support me whatever I choose but to make sure it's the right move for me."

"Can I have a look at what you've got written down so far?" Holly asks.

"Sure." I hand her the notebook while I tuck into the soup. It tastes as good as it smells.

"These are fantastic ideas, and I wouldn't have thought of half the stuff you have wrote down. I'll leave you to it. Enjoy the soup." and Holly goes back towards the kitchen.

After finishing my soup and writing down some more thoughts, I'm about to head up to my room when Hunter walks in. Hoping that he hasn't seen me, I put my head down to make it look like I'm busy so hopefully he won't come over to me.

"Emma, can I sit down?" Hunter asks with his hand on the back of the chair opposite.

"I was just going." I start to get up.

"Please, I won't keep you long," Hunter pleads.

"Fine." I sit back down.

"I swear that it is over between me and Lana. It was before I moved here. Yes, we talked about marriage, but in the end, she wasn't the person I wanted to spend my life with. We were happy for a while. In the end, I wasn't happy in New York; it wasn't the live that I thought we would have. She was always busy either with work or her friends. Everything that we did was her decision, and I didn't want to live like that. I tried talking to her about it, but she said I was imagining everything. I was being made redundant and my Aunt Holly wanted some help, so I thought it was the perfect time to move back home. It's what I wanted in the end to be home. City life isn't for me. I was thinking Lana would come with me as she loves me, but she wouldn't. She just didn't love me enough to be where I needed to be. I didn't see any of this until I lost my job, which made me consider things."

"Why did she turn up last night? Why does she think you are still together?"

"She had gotten into her head that the only reason we weren't together was because she didn't move with me. I've spent the day telling her that it is over, that it was over ages ago, that we aren't meant to be. I still care for her, but I don't love her. Since meeting you, I know what true love is. What I feel for you is way more than I ever felt for Lana. She has gotten the message now and is going back to New York tomorrow. She isn't even going to rent the salon here now, as it's not what she really wants; it never was. She found out I had brought I shop and was hoping to persuade me to give it to her for her salon. I can't do that. This is my dream. This is my chance to be who I am meant to be. She is selfish and I can't believe it took me as long as it did to see that. I was so unhappy in New York. If I had seen it earlier, I would have saved myself a lot of heartache."

"That is a lot to take in. Why didn't you tell me about her?"

"I could say we hadn't really talked about it, but there have been chances for me to tell you and I'm truly sorry that I didn't. I guess I was hoping we had time for that conversation."

"Why did she stay at your place last night?" I can't get this thought out of my head that he let her stay.

"It was late. I couldn't just kick her out."

"Why not? Didn't that send her the wrong signal. Where is she staying tonight?" I didn't need him to answer. His face said it all. She was staying with him again.

"There is no room at the hotel, and I didn't think her staying here is a good idea."

"Yea, you said as much this morning. I'm tired." I pick up my notebook and pen and go to my room without another word or hearing any more from Hunter. I think I've listened enough for today. I need to process all this information.

#

Chapter Seventeen

I'm off to Burlington today and I'm going to enjoy myself and not think about Hunter, not too much anyway. Today is about getting a real feel for the surrounding area to see if I can make the move. I have come to the conclusion that Hunter is telling me the truth; Lana seems like a real piece of work. I couldn't imagine asking Hunter to turn the bookshop into a salon. The thing that is sticking with me, though, is that he has let her stay at his place for two nights. I know it might seem silly to be hung up on that bit, but if there were truly no feelings there, then he would have turned her away, especially for the second night. Anyway, enough of Hunter, I'm going exploring. I get a taxi to take me into Burlington.

From there, I go to Lake Champlain. There is a lovely view of the lake, and it looks so peaceful. It's bright blue in the sunlight. The aromas give you the feeling of being at a beach. There are boats of different sizes moored along the waterfront. It is beautiful, and I can imagine it on a hot summers day making a wonderful walk. I could diffidently come here often; there is something about the water that is calming. I spend an hour walking along enjoying the view, letting my mind wonder and the water calm me. I have to admit now, though, that it is colder along here by the water.

I go in search of Church Street Marketplace, where Holly said is a great place for shopping. They have a fabulous big tree at one end and trees that lead up to it. These are covered in lights which must look spectacular in the evenings. There are a lot of historical buildings along here that have been preserved, so they look as beautiful now as they did when they were built. The street is longer than I was expecting; it is full of shops of all varieties, from big names to local businesses. I can't wait to go and explore. I love shopping, what girl doesn't. I have to just remember that I don't have much free room left in my luggage.

I have a wonder up and down, making mental notes of which shops I want to look in. Then, I head off for a spot of lunch at a lovely cafe on the corner. Afterwards, I go back to the stores that I wanted to have a good look around. One of those being Frog Hollow where local artists sell their work. Most of the artwork is really nice, some not so much but that is my opinion, as I don't like abstract art.

My favourite shop has to be Lake Champlain Chocolates; the smell is outstanding. Chocolate mixed with sweetness; it draws you to the big display cabinet, showcasing all the different flavours. You can buy readymade boxes or make up your own. They also have bars of different types, strawberries dipped in chocolate and round bars shaped like pizza. I treated myself with some luxury chocolates for later.

The last shop I go to is Slate, where I get myself a little souvenir. There is so much choice; it's amazing what can be carved or put on slate. I get myself a state shape Vermont, which has Vermont engraved inside it. I also get a lovely slab of slate that has a painted scene of the lake. I think my mum will love it.

I get coffee and go to Battery Park. I want to soak up some history while I'm here. It has a lovely view of the lake and the distant Adirondack Mountains. It's a view that you wouldn't get board of looking at; it must be a fabulous picnic area in the summer. There is an ice rink, which I'm thinking is an American thing, as they seem to have them everywhere during the winter. After a while, I go for a wander around the park and come across a totem pole of the Whispering Giant. It's a wonderful carved wooden structure. I then come across the military statue of a civil war cavalry officer called William Wells. There is a lot of history in this park, as I find out when I come across the tablet that has been put up in commemoration of the defence of Burlington during the war of 1812.

I've enjoyed learning about the history of Burlington even if it's only the small amount that I have learnt today. I would enjoy coming back here to learn more and see more of its history if I do move.

#

By late afternoon, I head back to Mistletoe and get out of the taxi the café so I can get myself something to take back to the inn. I've had a good time in Burlington and would be happy with all that on my doorstep. The longer I'm here and the more I think about it, the more I do want to move here. It's a once-in-a-lifetime chance. I don't think this opportunity will come again. Also, the job with Holly is perfect. I know I won't get anything that good back home.

As I walk past the bookshop, Hunter is closing it.

"Emma, hi. How was your day?" Hunter asks.

"Hi, Hunter. It was great. How are you getting on?"

"Not too bad. Walls are finished, so I have to just put everything back. How did you like Burlington?"

"That's good. The lake is beautiful, and I can imagine it in the summer as a popular destination."

"It is. Did you go to the marketplace?"

"I sure did. I looked in a few shops and admired some others. Got some chocolate to have later," I say, holding up my shopping bags.

"From Lake Champlain Chocolates? They are divine from there. You will enjoy them."

"They certainly smell and look delicious. I could have brought half the shop."

"I love their whiskey truffles and their salted caramel dark chocolate."

"I got their milk chocolate praline truffles and gin selection. I thought they'd go nice sitting in front of the fire and reading."

"That sounds like a good plan. I'm glad we are talking again."

"Me too."

"Holly told me about the job she has offered you. It sounds amazing."

"It's a wonderful opportunity, but I haven't decided if I'm taking it yet."

"For what it counts, I hope you decide to take the job," Hunter says, giving me half a smile.

"Hunter," I start, but he interrupts me.

"Emma, I'm really sorry about Lana showing like she did, but I had no idea she was going to do that. Or that she had it in her head that we could still be together," he pleads.

"That's not what I'm upset about. I believe you on that front."

"Then what it is?" he asks, confused.

"Really?" I say aspirated.

"Because Lana stayed at mine?" he asks.

"Yes. Surely you see why that is a problem?" I say, feeling agitated.

"She had nowhere else to stay. What was I meant to do?"

"That might have been the case for the first night but not the second. You could have sent her somewhere."

"Did you want her to be here where you are?"

"That would have sent the right message, even if I didn't want her here. You said you loved me. I was ready to move for you. Now, I don't know how I feel about it all."

"Nothing happened between us," he says.

"I believe that, but you don't see that having your ex-fiancé staying with you as a problem. I don't know where that leaves us."

"I don't either, but I don't want to give up on us. Let me take you out for some food and see if we can get back to how we were."

"I am hungry, but I'm not promising anything."

We go to the pub and order food. We have hardly spoken two words to each other since leaving. The atmosphere is tense, but once the food arrives, we settle into a rhythm of chatter and things feel like they used to.

"Is Lana one of the reasons you moved to New York?" I shouldn't bring her back up, but I need to know.

"Yes. This is why I keep telling you that you need to make the decision to move for you. As much as I would love for you to move here, I wouldn't ask you to. I don't want you to come to regret the decision and me."

"Do you regret your move?"

"I'm glad I did, but I stayed there as long as I did for Lana."

"Do you resent her for that?"

"I did, but that was before I realised that we were wrong for each other. In New York, everything was about Lana and what she wanted to do. It just took me a while to open my eyes to that fact."

"They do say love is blind."

"They do. I don't love her anymore. I love you. My feelings for you are far more that what I ever felt for Lana."

"I understand now why you haven't actually asked me to move here." I did wonder why.

"I should have explained sooner. I'm sorry. For what's it's worth, the offer from Holly is a fantastic one. I may not know the work side of you, but from what you have told me, this is a great opportunity for you."

"It is, yes, and if it were at home, I wouldn't be finding it this hard to make my mind up. Like you said, I have to make this the right choice for me."

I'm starting to think that I might have overreacted, but I can't help how I felt. I'm glad Hunter told me all this. It has given me a better understanding of him.

Now that I've let it go, things feel like they were. He is easy to be around, like I've always thought. We just click and it feels like we have known each other for years, not days. Life is tough, though, as nothing is ever perfect. No relationship is. Maybe we rushed into it too quickly. If it was just a holiday romance, I wouldn't mind, but we both know that's it's more than that. By the time we have finished our meal, things between us have gone back to how they were. I think we just need to take it slower if I stay. Reminding me of the decision that I need to make, but I will make it for me and not to stay to be with Hunter; that will just be a bonus. We walk back to the inn, holding hands. Hunter only kisses me goodbye on the cheek, which was perfect, like he knew what I was thinking.

#

Chapter Eighteen

New Year's Eve has arrived and I'm feeling at peace. Last night, I felt good being out with Hunter. I'm still considering the job offer and inching more to accepting it, but I don't want to say anything yet, as I want to be one hundred percent sure. It would be hard not being able to drive to go and see family and friends, but I would make new friends. We can fly out to each other, too. It will be the adventure of a lifetime to move out here and the job is what dreams are made of. Am I being silly, even thinking about taking it? It's so far from home and I would be all alone except Holly and Hunter. Then again, I am young and can make a life for myself here—one I have only dreamed about. I'm going mad, going over and over it all in my head.

I take myself out for a walk to clear my head. I'm glad Holly isn't constantly asking me if I have made up my mind. She knows it's a big decision and that I will tell her once I have finally decided. As I walk around the town, people are busy taking supplies to the community centre for the big party later. It's meant to be big, with most of the town expected to turn up. There will be food available that is supplied by the townspeople themselves. You can take along your own booze, as all that will be supplied is soft drinks. It sounds like a wonderful community event, which I'm looking forward to attending.

"Emma!" Someone shouts from outside the centre.

"Yes?" I say, unsure who the gentleman is and how he knows who I am.

"My name's Tony. I'm the chair of the community council and in charge of tonight's festivities. Holly told us that you are an event planner?" Tony explains.

"That's right," I say, shaking his hand.

"We are in dire need of some assistance. The lady who had the whole thing planned has fallen ill. She didn't make any notes, as it's all up here she was always saying," he says, pointing to his head. I've met quite a few people like that.

"What can I help with?" I say, happy to help.

"Any time you can spare to direct people as to where to put things, or they will just end up anywhere."

"OK, shall we go in," I say already on my way inside.

Tony was right when he said dire, there are random tables here and there. The lights are just strung up in no order at all. Taking my coat off, I ask Tony for a clipboard, paper and pen. Then, I take stock of the room and what supplies I can see and set about drawing out a rough plan.

I get the food tables moved to the far wall and the tall tables set out in front of those, leaving space for a clear dance floor, which no one seemed to have thought about. After that, I set about getting the lights hung in a nicer order. There is no shortage of help here, which is good because we don't have long as people need to go and cook and get ready themselves. Last on my list are the Happy New Year decorations.

"Have you thought about taking the Christmas decorations down from walls and ceiling to give it more a new-year vibe? Keep the tree, as it is still the festive season," I ask Tony.

"I didn't think of that. Do we have time?" Tony says, looking at his watch.

"We should do if everyone can stay an extra half an hour." I think it will make all the difference to the feel of the party.

Most people do stay and we manage to get the decorations down and away by 5 pm. I'm just putting the last box away when I spot some silver tablecloths.

"Do you use these on the tables?" I ask Tony.

"No, we tend to leave them plain."

"Would you mind if I use them just on the tall tables where spills are less likely? It will add to the vibe of the party."

"I don't see why not." Tony says merrily.

I'm happy with the final look. The tablecloths set off the grown-up atmosphere of the evening. All they need is some tea lights in the middle. I will ask Holly if there are any at the inn that can be used. There isn't much decoration, but by taking down the Christmas ones and putting up more lights, it sets of the right atmosphere for a new year party.

"Thank you, Emma. They look great and really set of the tables," Tony says, looking around the room.

"You're welcome. I couldn't just leave the tables bare." I'm happy that Tony likes them. He likes my idea for candles and says I can just bring them with me when I come later.

Holly is in reception when she got back.

"I hope I didn't put you on the spot today with Tony," Holly says as I walk in.

"No, of course not. It was good to have a project, kept my mind of things. I don't suppose you have any spare tea lights that can go on the tables at the party?"

"I think I do. Let me go and check."

Holly is soon back with a box of tea lights for me. "Thanks, Holly. I best go and get ready."

"See you down here for pre-party drinks in a bit."

With that, I head back to my room to give Mum a ring before getting ready to party. I have reached my decision, so I need to speak to my mum about it right away.

"Happy New Year, Mum."

"Happy New Year, Love. Have you come to the decision?" Mum asks, eager to know.

"I have, I think. I hope I'm making the right one." I'm starting to doubt my choice.

"Have you made it for yourself?"

"Yes, I have."

"Then it's the right decision," Mum says encouragingly.

"Thanks, Mum."

"Come on, don't keep me in suspense."

"I want to move here. It's a dream job and I can see myself living here and being happy. As long as you will be OK and are happy for me to move."

"Of course, I'm happy for you. I don't want to stand in the way of your dreams. I am sad for me, but we will still see each other and talk all the time. Have you told Holly?"

"Not yet. I wanted to talk to you first."

"How about things with Hunter, have they improved?"

"They have a bit. We are going to the party together, but I want to take things slower. I think maybe we rushed things."

"That's make sense. You are in no rush. Enjoy your party and I will see you in a couple of days."

"I'll see you in a few days, Mum. Have a goodnight."

"Bye, love."

I'm on top of the world while I'm getting ready. I'm happy with my decision and feel better about it now that I have talked to my mum. I sing in the shower and dance my way into my dress. I take my time doing my hair, curling it and putting half of it up. By the time I've finished, I feel a million dollars in my glittery silver dress and high heels. I pick up my snow boots. I don't want to walk there in heels; that's just asking for trouble. I head downstairs to where Holly is doing the pre-party drinks.

Holly has set up a makeshift bar in the dining area with a variety of alcohol and cocktail shakers. She has even made her own cocktail, which she is busy making up for people to try. She has hung up a few new year decorations, too. The cocktail has a kick to it, but once you get past that, it's actually quite nice. She has also got some pizzas out so that everyone can help themselves and line their stomachs with food. Which I'm glad for, I didn't think about food. It's a lovely, relaxed atmosphere with laughter and chatter with everyone looking really happy and dressed to the nines in their best clothes. Hunter walks in and says his hellos before coming over to me and kisses me on the check.

"You look absolutely stunning, Emma." I'm pretty sure I'm blushing.

"Thank you. You don't look so bad yourself." Admiring Hunter's suit minus the tie. He looks breath-taking. I'm so glad he is my date.

"Is that one of Aunt Holly's famous cocktails?" he says, nodding at my drink.

"Famous?" I query.

"Yea, for being overly strong. One drink can knock you off your feet," he says with laughter.

"I'll bear that in mind and just have this one, then," I say, taking another sip of my drink. I don't want to get drunk before midnight at least.

#

After an hour, Holly boxes up the remaining pizza slices and we all head to the centre. There is cheer from everyone on their way to the party, making the atmosphere a joyful one. I've remembered the candles and I put them on the tables while Holly puts the pizza on the food table. People are already mingling, and the food table is overflowing with goodies. Praises are being said with how the room looks and that makes me feel good with more people talking to me and making me feel welcome.

The party soon gets going with people dancing, chatting and eating. It feels like one big family celebrating together; it's the best night. I know that I'm making the right choice. Being here with everyone being friendly has confirmed that for me. I'm feeling excited and can't wait to tell Holly, but maybe just not right now, as I'm a bit merry. Hunter and I have been getting on tonight, just like we had been, like the last couple of days didn't happen.

"Are you having a good night, Emma?" Holly asks as we take a breather from dancing.

"I am. It's amazing. I can't wait for this town to be my home," I blurt out.

"Does that mean you've decided to take the job?" Holly asks eagerly.

"It does, but let's keep it between us for tonight. I wasn't going to say anything, but it just came out."

We do a quick toast before anyone sees and then Holly goes off to talk to some other people. I'm feeling on top of the world as the clock gets near midnight.

"You look really happy. It's nice to see," Hunter says as he strokes a hand down my face.

"I am. I'm looking forward to starting a new year with new challenges."

"I hope you get everything you want in the New Year. It's going to be a busy year for me with opening the bookstore, but I can't wait."

"It's going to be amazing. Just like this whole trip has been and I get to end it with a bang."

At midnight, we share a magical kiss and dance in each other's arms. The rest of the evening is spent giving and receiving well wishes, more dancing and drinking. Hunter doesn't leave my side after midnight. At the end of the night, everyone from the inn walks back together so that we can support each other on the walk back. It is quite the sight to see, with loads of laughter and near misses of people slipping. That is the sign of a good night out.

#

Chapter Nineteen

It's a late start for New Year's Day and I'm glad that Holly is doing breakfast late. I'm feeling a little sensitive this morning. I take a bit longer than normal to get ready, allowing the shower to revitalise me. It was a fantastic night last night; I feel ready for the move and that I will be accepted as one of the community. Downstairs, some of the guests are already going about their day; they must be feeling better that I do. I'm about to get a table when I spot Hunter seating at one, eating his breakfast.

"Morning," I say as I take a seat opposite him.

"Morning." He smiles back.

"Didn't want to do your own breakfast this morning?" I say, nodding at his plate.

"Well, after walking you back last night Aunt Holly said I could crash here, so I did. Plus, her breakfasts are the best."

"Yes, they are. I'm so hungry." My tummy rumbles right on Que. Just then, Holly comes and takes my order and brings me a cup of coffee.

"How's your head this morning?" Holly asks me.

"A bit hung over, but a full breakfast will help."

"How's your memory of last night?" Holly asks me with an eyebrow raised.

"My memory is perfect." I reply, trying to convey that I remember telling her that I will take the job. She then goes off to make my breakfast.

"What was that about?" asks Hunter.

"Nothing. Did you have a good time last night?" I'm not ready to tell him just yet.

"I did. The best parts were spent with you in my arms."

"I liked that bit, too. Who knew you could dance."

"I'm not that bad," he says laughing.

When my food arrives, there is silence. We share lingering looks and we're touching each other foots under the table. It feels like it did at the start with sparks between us. I can't wait to move out here and see where this goes. We sit there for a while, drinking more coffee and just enjoying the moment.

#

"Emma, have you got a moment?" Holly asks, after clearing her throat.

"Yea, sure," I say, dragging my eyes from Hunter's.

"I should probably go home to change. I'll see you later," Hunter says.

"Shall we go to my office?" Holly says. Once we are there and sitting down, Holly asks, "Did you mean what you said last night?"

"I did mean it, yes."

"Are you sure? Have you thought about it thoroughly? And you are doing this for you? Sorry a lot of questions, but I want to make sure," Holly asks, bombarding me with questions.

"Where to start. Right, I have thought about nothing else, so yes I'm sure, and I am defiantly doing it just for me," I say brightly, a huge smile on my face.

"I'm so excited for you to be part of my next adventure. Have you told Hunter?"

"Not yet. Thanks for not saying anything in front of him. I want to surprise him with it later. I thought it was better to make it official first."

"I didn't want to overstep with not being sure if he knows or not. I'm happy to see you two are getting on again."

"We are, thank you. I'm excited to see where it goes."

"Let's get down to business, then. With you going home tomorrow, we need to discuss some details that I need, and I thought maybe you could do some stuff back at home."

"No problem."

"Do you think you could set up a website and social media while your home and come up with detailed plans for events. I'm hoping for the barn to be built and ready by summer."

"That is all doable from home and I should be here way before the barn is finished."

"I need all your details for your visa application. I can help with it and together we will get you here as soon as."

We spend the next couple of hours going over all the information that we both need. We will be able to communicate through teams and share documents. We are both enthusiastic about the future and come out the office smiling and laughing. I can tell this is going to be great and we get on so well, which is good as we will be working closely together.

#

After leaving Holly, I go up to my room to pack. Holly, has said that I can leave some stuff here to save on weight.

Plus, I would only be bringing it back. I should go and see Hunter and tell him, but I want to keep it to myself for a while longer. I'm over the moon at the prospect of a whole new life here. I just hope it doesn't take too long to get me back. It doesn't take me long to pack now, as I only need to take the essentials with me.

I'm glad I have stuff to be getting on with while at home. It will keep me busy and keep me up to date with the workload. I want this adventure to be successful for Holly and me. I don't want to let her down. Also, once I'm home, I will have to sort through all my things, what to bring and what to leave. That will be a big task. More importantly than both of those, though, will be to spend as much time as I can with my family. They are what I'm going to miss the most, but I know they support my choices and will come and visit.

#

After an hour, I go in search of Hunter. He's not at home, so I go to the shop and find him there. Looking in the window, I can see him looking at something long.

"I've been looking for you. What's that you are looking at?" I ask.

"Oh, urm, it's the sign I had made. I wanted you to see it before you went, then Lana showed up and it didn't feel right hanging it, so I just left it inside," he says, looking at his shoes.

"Can I see it now?"

"Sure." He moves to the side so that I can see the whole thing.

"It looks great. I'm glad you liked my name and slogan. It looks good at the bottom. The mistletoe on the ends is a nice touch, too." It's only then that I notice that the shop has been put back together and it looks wonderful. The bunting that I brought him is hanging on the counter and looks perfect. "When did you do all this?"

"While we weren't talking. I wanted to be able to show it you before you left."

"I love what you've done with the place. I can't wait to see it full of people," I say with a sly smile to see if he notices my use of wording.

"See it? Wait, have you decided to take the job?"

"I have. That's what Holly wanted me for this morning. We were discussing what happens next."

Hunter then picks me up and twirls me around, then kisses me passionately. The first proper kiss since Lana showed up. It's full of love, it's magical.

"Take it. That means you're happy I'm coming back?"

"Are you kidding? I'm overjoyed that you are coming back." He kisses me again, slower this time.

"We still need to build on trust, but I can't wait to see what the future holds for us."

"Neither can I."

We spend a couple of hours together before I need to head back to the inn to make sure I have everything I need from Holly. Hunter says he wants to do a couple of things, but he will see me later at the inn. I'm so excited about the future. My flight isn't till tomorrow afternoon, so there is no rush in the morning, which will make the goodbyes easier. Hunter is going to stop at the inn so that will make things easier, but harder at the same time. I have to keep telling myself that I will be back. Plus, we will talk on the phone while I'm home.

I'm on my way downstairs when I hear voices, but more than usual, so I walk cautiously. It looks like half the town has come to the inn, but I don't know why. I don't remember there being anything on tonight. Wanting to know what is going on, I search the crowd for Holly.

"Holly, what's happening. Why are there so many people here?"

"Emma, just the person," she answers and takes my hand and leads me to by the fireplace. Picking up the microphone that is on hand, she says, "Ladies and gentlemen, can I have your attention please. Thank you all for coming. As many of you know, I have been looking to expand and take on an events manager. With the Christmas season being busy, the look for one was put on hold; that was until I realised that I had the perfect candidate staying with me. She loves our little town and Christmas just as much as all us residents do, plus she has taken a shine to my fabulous nephew, which is very much reciprocated, I might add. She has decided to move over here from her home in Wales and be my events manager. So, I would like to propose a toast to Emma. She is leaving us for a bit tomorrow but will be back full of ideas for events to be held here, so here's to Emma!" She raises her glass and so does everyone else.

Hunter was passing the glasses around while the speech was going on, finally giving one to his aunt and one to me.

"Thank you for your kind words. Holly, I am looking forward to coming back here and starting a new chapter in my life. All of you have been so kind since my arrival and made me feel at home. I know that I'm going to be very happy here," I say with Hunter at my side.

"You didn't have to this, Holly," I say once the general chit chat has continued.

"It's the least I could do. Plus, I had help. You have made quite the impression here," she says, then excuses herself to go and talk to someone else.

"Did you know about this?" I ask Hunter.

"I did. It was my idea to do something for you tonight, but it's Holly who made it into this," he says, waving his arms around.

"Well, thank you." I give him a kiss on the check. We then go and mingle.

It's a wonderful impromptu party with food laid out in the dining room. It's amazing what people can do in a small amount of time. I'm overwhelmed by the number of people who are here to wish me well. A lot of them are intrigued by what I am planning on doing, as well as giving me some ideas of their own. I make a mental note of the good ideas in which there are few. They will go a long way to bring more people into the town, which is always a good thing.

The atmosphere is a relaxed one with gentle music playing in the background; no one seems to be up for a lot of drinking after last night. The food is delicious, and the evening soon goes with many needing an early night to catch up on some sleep. Me, Hunter and Holly end the night with mugs of hot chocolate curled up in front of the fire.

#

Chapter Twenty

It's the day of going home. I wake with a mixture of feelings, happy to be seeing my family, yet sad to be leaving. This place is home now; I can feel it in my heart. I start to think of it as not really going home, just going to see my family. This thought makes my smile even more. I roll over and kiss Hunter good morning.

An hour later, we head downstairs for some breakfast, my last American breakfast for a while, so I go the whole hog. Felling extremely stuffed, we go out for a walk so that I can see the town for one last time. It's an emotional walk and I take my time so that I can see as much as I can before I have to leave.

"I will miss you," Hunter says, giving me a goodbye hug.

"I will miss you, too. Good luck with opening the bookstore." He opens it in two days.

"Thank you and thank you for your help with it."

"Holly, are you sure it's OK me leaving most of my things here?" I turn to Holly, double checking for the hundredth time.

"It's fine. Stop worrying. It makes more sense to leave it here that you to take it and bring it back," she says, giving me a hug.

"I will work hard and be in touch all the time."

"I have faith that you will. Don't work all the time, though; you spend time with your family and friends. You will be back before you know it."

We wave bye as I get in the taxi. I'm trying not to cry; I didn't think I would be this emotional. It goes to show what they mean to me and what the place does.

My flight home is uneventful: lots of sleeping and reading the new book that Hunter gave me. I plan to call a taxi from the airport, and I'm surprised to see that my mum has come to pick me up.

"I wasn't expecting you to pick me up, Mum," I say as I give her a hug.

"I've missed you and couldn't wait to hear all about it till you got home." She has tears in her eyes, which make mine water too.

"Missed you, too."

"Shall we get a coffee before the drive back?" Mum asks.

"Sounds wonderful, Mum."

I tell her all about the town while we have coffee. In the car, we talk about Hunter and my new job. Mum seems generally happy for me, which is good. I was worried a bit. She says she has lots planned for the next couple of weeks, as she has taken time of work. I'm looking forward to it all. This year is my year; I can feel it. Dreams really do come true.

They also come with a lot of paperwork. I was expecting a fair amount that I would need to fill in but not this much. I'm so grateful to Holly for sponsoring my visa, as it is making it a bit easier to sort out. I've also had to sort out with her what benefits I would be getting, as I need to sort out health insurance. It's a lot to get my head around because it is so different from here because we have the NHS.

Sorting through my things is a bigger task than I thought it would, as shipping fees are expensive. Luckily, I don't have much and I left my things over there so I'm hoping to just get away with my baggage allowance. Mum has said she will give me some money so I can buy more winter clothes once I'm out there.

Mum keeps taking my mind off all the paperwork with days out. We have been to the Zoo and a couple of castles. She wants me to take in all the local history and sites and we are creating a scrapbook of our time together. It's fun and emotional at the same time. Sometimes I feel as if Mum thinks she won't see me again and I keep reminding that we will, and I'll be ringing her a lot. It is hard though, as we both now know no matter how much we say we will see a lot of each other that it will be hard. America is a long way and not always cheap flights.

"Thanks for all the days out, Mum. They have been wonderful."

"You're welcome, love, and they have, haven't they? I've had such a lovely time."

"You didn't have to arrange all these days out, though. Not that I'm not grateful."

"I know, but I thought it would be better for us to be out and about making memories that sitting in the house waiting for you to go."

"I'm going to miss you, Mum."

"Met, too, love."

We give each other a hug and when we pull apart, we both have tears in our eyes. This really is going to be hard. It really has been wonderful getting out and it definitely helps pass the time while I'm waiting on paperwork.

It takes a few months to sort out all the paperwork. I have been doing some work for Holly. I have set up an events page on the website and added some events into the calendar already for this year. I've been enjoying the work and look forward to more of it when I get out there. I've got a wedding booked for the summer, which will be the first one. I'm so excited to get stuck into the planning. We will be having an Autumn, I mean Fall, I need to get used to that, festival. Bigger Christmas plans. We also have a couple of parties starting to book with us; this is really going to be exciting and profitable for Holly.

On me and Hunter, we have been talking a lot and getting to know each other more, which is great. My heart and body ache to see him in the flesh, though. He is doing well with his bookstore and getting busier. I think once I'm out there, our relationship will soon blossom into the real thing. He has been commissioned to illustrate for a children's book, which is fabulous. I'm so proud of him for following through with it. He needs to do what makes him happy after years of doing what his ex wanted.

I've discovered new places that will be local that I can't wait to see. Ben and Jerry's factory is in Waterbury Vermont, and you can have a tour of the factory, followed by lots of ice cream. It was their first factory, and it was built in 1985, with tours starting a year later. I'm looking forward to trying new flavours that we don't get here in Wales. There are a few museums that I would love to visit at some point, too.

On my last night, my family and friends have thrown me a leaving party. It's overwhelming but in a good way, all my extended family is here as well as my old work friends and friends in general. It's good to be able to say bye to them all.

Some I might not see again, but I know the important ones will come to America. We have fun dancing and laughing together.

"Thank you for this wonderful party. I've laughed and cried, but all in good fortune. I'm lucky to be able to go and live my dream. I wouldn't be strong enough to, without all the support from you, lovely people. Thank you to everyone's advice and the generous gifts. I will keep in touch with you all and we will see each other from time to time. I'm going to miss you all. Let's get back to dancing, shall we." I hate giving speeches, but this occasion called for one.

The gifts I have received are dollars, as everyone knows I don't have much room in my luggage. Some of my closet friends have given me picture books of our fun times together, which I'm grateful for. It will be good to have these memories with me.

"Have you had a good time, love?" Mum asks me once we get home.

"I have. Thank you." I give her a hug.

"We all wanted to show you how much you will missed and that we all fully support you."

"I'm glad you will be coming out to me for Christmas. You're going to love it there." I was so happy when Mum said that she wants to spend Christmas in Mistletoe with me.

"I'm looking forward to it. You will be nice and settled by then. It will be nice to see where you are living and that you have settled well."

"I will have the whole trip planned. You will get to meet Hunter, too, if things are still going well."

"I'm sure they will be. It will be nice to see him in person and not just on a tiny screen."

"You really are the best, Mum. I'm going to miss you loads."

"I'll miss you, too."

It's a tearful goodbye in the morning, but I'm also filled with joy for my adventure ahead.

#

Epilogue

It was late spring when I got back to Mistletoe. It was hard not seeing Hunter all that time, but I also think it did us some good, too. It made us get our feelings in order and I'm happy to say that they have grown stronger. We spend all our free time together and I have even met his parents who live in Maine. It's a lovely place, but I do prefer Mistletoe and Burlington.

The lake is as beautiful in the summer as I imagined it would be. Hunter took me on a boat ride so I could see it from a different perspective. It was wonderful and I'm looking forward to doing it again. I've done more exploring the history of the place. It's lovely in the summer too, as it was in the winter. I have been on many hiking sessions through lush greenery, with amazing views. I got to on the Ben and Jerry's factory tour. There were so many new flavours to try, new to me at least.

I am glad that I made the move, as it has been amazing since the first day I got here. I now live with Hunter and that is perfect. I enjoyed living at the inn, but it is nice to be able to be away from it and switch off from work. Hunter's book shop is going really well. He has had an author event that went well. I'm so proud of him. He is also doing great with illustrating and getting another gig. He really is an amazing artist.

I was able to see the barn being finished and put in some last details that I thought should be there. I have come up with lots of ideas and implemented quite a few of them. We have more going on this Christmas, which will make it mad around here. Today, I'm setting up for our first wedding to be held in the barn. There is an archway filled with cream flowers of a wide variety, where the couple will say their vows. White chairs make up the isle with flowers at the end of each set. The rest of the barn is filled with fairy lights and more flowers, as well as gold organza hung across the ceiling. It looks amazing; everyone has worked hard to get it like this.

"There you are," Hunter says, putting his arms around me.

"Just making sure that everything is in order," I say before kissing him.

"It looks very romantic. I'm sure the bride and groom will be happy. Speaking of which some guests have started to arrive."

"I best go and greet them."

"Aunt Holly can do that for a minute. I wanted to talk to you."

"But it's my job to greet them," I say, trying to leave.

"Emma," Hunter says, grabbing my hand.

"OK. One minute."

Hunter holds my hand and leads me down the aisle. I'm wondering what he is up to, especially if the guest are arriving. We are standing in the archway, and he lets go of my hand and drops down to one knee. I gasp, not believing my eyes.

"Emma. You make me the happiest man alive; you complete me. I thought I knew what love was until I met you and released that I didn't have a clue. These past ten months of getting to know, you have the best of my life. We may not have been together long, but when you know, you know. Life is short and I want to spend the rest of mine with you as my wife. Emma, will you marry me?"

"Yes." It's all I can say, as I'm lost for words. I wasn't expecting this. Maybe at some point, but not right now. We kiss under the arch for a long time when we are interrupted by a cough.

"Congratulations, you two, but can I have my event manager back for a bit. There is a wedding happening today," says Holy from the doorway.

"Sorry, Holly. I'm on my way."

"No need to be sorry. I brought you as much time as I could, but the bride would like to see the barn before she goes and gets ready. You have done a spectacular job, Emma," Holly says, looking around.

"We will celebrate later; I really do have to go," I say to Hunter, letting go of him.

"It's fine. I was going to wait till later, but then I saw this place, I thought this looks like a perfect place to propose. I couldn't wait any longer to ask you. I'm sure the bride won't mind."

I go and greet the bride, looking at my finger all the way there. It's a gorgeous ring, white gold with one big diamond that is surrounded by smaller ones. I can't believe that just happened and now I have to carry on working. I'm over the moon. Not only have I got my American dream with a dream job, but I have the dream guy too. Never give up on your dreams.

The End